PEN & INK
SHORT STORY
BOOK

BY

Assorted Authors

A series of short stories from the
Pen & Ink Designs Publishing
Writing Competitions

Copyright © Pen & Ink Designs Publishing 2024
Originally published 2014
Images/Cover © Pen & Ink Designs Publishing 2024

ISBN - 9781915086174
Edition 2

Publisher: Pen & Ink Designs Publishing

www.penandinkdesigns.co.uk

CONTENTS

* * * * *

MESSAGE TO OUR READERS

We hope you enjoy reading this updated version of the original Pen & Ink Designs Short Story Book. The assortment of stories in the original version has been enhanced and edited for your reading enjoyment.

Please be aware that the writers of these works come from countries across the world. As such, you will find there will be some variations in the spelling of the English language used. Please take the spelling as being correct for the author who wrote the story and the country they are from.

Thank you for your understanding.

THE END OF
A HEROINE

'Extract from the Grantham Gazette'

30th September 2012:

Scourge of the supermarket Shirley Smith dies, aged 78. Yesterday, residents of Pumley Green expressed their sadness at the death of their most famous resident, Shirley Smith, who last week died peacefully in her own home.

Smith, a quiet lady, gained nationwide fame when she came up against increasing pressure from her local council to sell her house to make way for a new building development. The development, which was to include the building of a large supermarket, would have meant the demolition of Smith's house, along with those of her neighbours.

In a battle reminiscent of David and Goliath the diminutive Smith refused to sell even when offered increasing amounts of money. Speaking a year before her death, she said, "My parents bought this house in the 1920s. I was born in one of the *bedrooms and I've lived here all my life. The house means more to me than money."*

In a landmark legal battle, Smith won her right to stay in her home and the nation celebrated her victory. "She was," remarked neighbour Alan Teasdale, "a true underdog. Her fight against the big companies meant she secured a place in our collective hearts. As a neighbour and a friend, I can confirm that she will be sadly missed."

20th September 2012

* * * * *

Alan Teasdale stepped out of his front door carrying a casserole dish in one hand and his front door keys in the other. For once, he was more preoccupied about what he was carrying than he was about the amount of litter clogging up his front garden. He did not notice the plastic bag currently strangling his gladioli.

Opening his front gate, he stood, looking first one way and then the other. His lip curled when he saw the lads hanging around at the end of the street. Some were sitting, whilst others were standing, half-heartedly dribbling a football between them.

'Why can't they get jobs? Or go to college?' he thought to himself. Anything to stop them being there - day in, day out.

One of his neighbours, Judith, slowly shuffled up to him.

"How are you, Judith?" he asked.

"I can't complain, although my hips are hurting me something terrible."

Alan nodded in sympathy, he knew all about Judith's hips.

"You been cooking?" Judith said, pointing to Alan's casserole dish.

"The missus has, aye."

"You taking it round to Miss Smith?"

"Aye."

"You taking care of her?"

"Aye"

"Well, somebody has to," and Judith began her slow shuffle down the street, towards the corner shop.

Alan did not watch her go. Instead, he turned and

entered his neighbour's front garden. Stepping over a chipped garden gnome, he rang the buzzer and waited. And he waited some more.

Eventually, he heard Shirley Smith making her slow way down the corridor to her front door.

"Good morning," he said brightly as the door opened.

"Good morning, Alan. Do come in."

Alan stepped through the doorway, onto a carpet that had not been changed since the 1960s. The pair made their way back down the corridor and into the sitting room. Every available space was covered with China, and the walls were covered with framed memorabilia. As usual, Alan found he couldn't take his eyes off it.

"Ah, yes, you like my cuttings, don't you, Alan?"

"Aye," he replied.

"My proudest moments."

Shirley settled into a chair, indicating that Alan should do the same. He sat down, knowing from experience that this would take some time.

Not too many people visited Shirley these days, so when she got him there, she liked to talk.

"Imagine, little old me on the front page of the Guardian,' she pointed at one of the framed cuttings, 'and there I am with Jeremy Paxman. Such a charming man."

Alan knew the script word for word. But still, Shirley would give him a tour of all the publicity she had received over her two-year battle to keep her, and the rest of them, on this street. He had heard it so many times that he knew it all off by heart.

As Shirley came to the end of her monologue, Alan was finally allowed to explain the reason for his visit.

"I've brought you over a meal," he said, holding up the casserole dish. "It's a stroganoff."

"Why, thank you, my dear."

"Shall I pop it in the kitchen?"

"Please," and she smiled at him.

"No need for you to get up. I can find my way," said Alan. "I'll put it in the fridge. All you need to do is heat it up."

After Alan had put the dish in the nearly empty fridge, he took a quick look around. Spying a set of keys, he picked them up and stuffed them in his pocket.

"I'll be off now, Shirley. Give us a shout if you need anything. I will be back in the next day or two to pick up the dish."

"Bye, my dear," called Shirley, smiling.

Alan let himself out and made his way back home.

His wife was waiting for him. "How did it go?"

"Fine."

"Do you think she'll eat it?"

"Aye."

"Did you get some keys?"

"Aye."

"So, you'll go and get the dish and clean up."

"I'll take care of everything. Stop worrying."

"Do you think it will work?"

"Aye," he paused for a moment and then added, "They're not called death cap mushrooms for nothing."

* * * * *

'Extract from the Grantham Gazette'

16th February 2013:

Pumley Green Development Gets the Go Ahead!

Exciting new plans for the development of the Pumley Green site were revealed today.

The controversial site, which has been dogged by bad press, has finally been given the go ahead. The complex will provide the town with a gym, a movie complex, exclusive living accommodations, a large supermarket, and a wide variety of eateries. It is estimated the development will generate around 800 new jobs.

A former resident of the now demolished houses, Alan Teasdale, said, "The area had been in a steady decline for many years, so we're thrilled to hear that it is finally going to be revitalised."

Asked if he was planning to move into one of the new apartments when they are finally built, Teasdale said, "The wife and I are really happy where we are now living so we won't be moving back to Pumley Green."

© **Christina Garbutt**

8

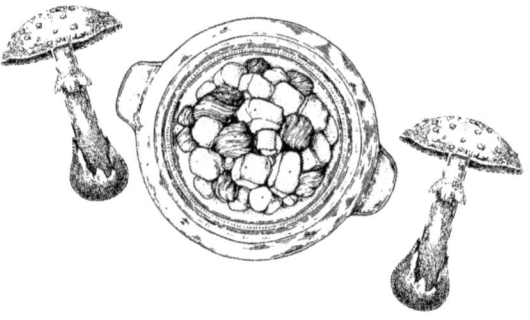

Images licensed to Pen & Ink Designs Publishing

WELTSCHMERZ

(Meaning – 'World Pain')

'He is known as Mr Sudsy — the washing powder tsar of Yorkshire.

People in the North-East were in awe of him; regarding him as the Donald Trump of detergent. The nexus of his empire was Hull, Grimsby, and Scunthorpe. Mr. Sudsy called it his soapy Bermuda Triangle. It was rumoured that his personal fortune is in excess of £25 million.'

Harold turned the page and continued to devour the fat police dossier:

'Mr. Sudsy likes to dress up as Vera Lynn and eat bridies (*) while prostitutes watch him masturbate. He claims to have slept with over 300 women. He is a sex addict, or as our generation likes to call it, 'a mad shagger.' Phil Minker, Soap Suds Regional Manager.'

The intercom on Harold's desk began to blink.

"Harold, Mrs. Marigold is on the phone, she's asking if she can make an emergency appointment with you this morning."

(*) Meat Pie or Pastry   9

Harold sighed. "I had three sessions with her last week; what's wrong with her now?"

"She says the voices have come back, and the begonia on her windowsill looks like Frank Bruno."

Harold groaned. "Book her in."

* * * * *

Harold assumed his favourite seat on the 5.15 p.m. express train to Hull. He opened his leather attaché case - the same one he had carried around for the last 25 years - and placed the Sudsy case file on his lap.

Where was he?

Ah, yes, page five. Mr. Sudsy had just abandoned his third wife and registered yet another business:

'Fishy Fries. Yorkshire's premier cod-flavoured snack. The fiasco was short-lived: Smiths, who owned Scampi Fries, initiated legal action, forcing Fishy Fries into a bumbling retreat. Mr Sudsy then retaliated by launching a range of Yorkshire-inspired sodas. The line included Red Bollocks and Miner's Yank, an energy drink containing burdock, mustard, and Guarana.'

Harold chuckled, attracting glances from the seat opposite.

Normally he would have been tangled in The Times crossword at this point. Somewhere between five across and an aneurysm, usually with a look of glazed resignation on his face.

The passenger opposite tried to glimpse the case file, but Harold, sensing the man's incursion, shifted his knee to shield the file with his grey flannel suit.

Eagerly scurrying to the appendix and wanting to find out what Mr Sudsy looked like, he was disappointed to find that the man in question was quite handsome. Not in the conventional sense, as he had dense, curly brown hair, ruddy cheeks, and a ten-bob smile. His clothes were Yorkshire Hollywood: chequered sports jacket, Paisley-pattern tie, and a pair of tan bell-bottoms.

If there was one thing that Harold's career had taught him, it was that most lotharios were not overly attractive. No, mainly because they usually relied on their psychological and vocal artillery. It also appeared that at the age of 14, Harold had discovered, to his eternal disappointment that girls went for silverback gorillas, not pseudointellectuals.

The man opposite once more attempted to peek over his spread-eagled newspaper, causing Harold to elevate his leg. This, in turn, brought an old-school photo of Mr. Sudsy into view. Immediately, he recognised the sallow paint of the school gymnasium wall. It couldn't be... could it?

Yes. Sat on the front bench, with his hands clasped on top of his scuffed knees, was a timid Harold. He was wedged between the future mayor of Grimsby and a local dermatologist. And there, grinning on the back row, was a young Mr Sudsy, surrounded by the class wags, sitting alongside his girlfriend, Jenny (the only girl in primary seven to have nurtured two hummocks under her school jumper).

He was shocked.

A sudden violent jolt shoogled (*) the train carriage, spraying the contents of the case file onto the floor.

The nosy stranger opposite immediately slipped off his seat, crouching on one knee, "Allow me to help."

"It's okay," blurted Harold, his grey face now flushed with emotion. "I can get them."

(*) shook, swayed, rocked   12

Unfortunately, in the subsequent fumble, the school photo had slipped under the seat, disappearing beneath the carriage heater.

The stranger continued to fuss.

"You know, we sit in the same carriage every day, but we never talk. I'm Nigel. I work for Barnaby and Joyce, Accountants in Grimsby."

"Harold, I work across the road at Sinker Psychiatry," he said reluctantly, shaking the man's hand. Then he scowled at the photo of Mr. Sudsy trapped under his left Hush Puppy.

* * * * *

The bus that shuttled between Hull train station and Harold's middle-class tomb of an office took around 40 minutes. Sitting on the top deck, he peered out at the muddy flats that flanked the River Ouse.

He wondered if the boy in the school photograph really was Mr Sudsy - the dolt who had incessantly teased him at school? Such parallels could be easily drawn by a 48-year-old man who, by virtue of age, would often find himself dissecting the past, rather than embracing the future. Mmm, he needed to think about that one.

Drawing a squeaky circle on the misted bus window, Harold peeked through the hole and saw his younger self playing tennis: strong, emerald eyes, palomino thighs, with a pinch of steel.

* * * * *

Later, holding a large Glenlivet, Harold, sat brooding in his study. His wife was next door, enjoying an episode of Lewis. The Sudsy file peeped out at him from his attaché case, but Harold was determined to ignore it, so he pretended to leaf through a periodical instead. Reading about Mr. Sudsy's life reduced him to a dreary whimper.

Suddenly, the phone on Harold's bureau began to jangle. It was his 'hotline,' the one his clients rang in the event of an implosion. Unfortunately, Mrs. Marigold had recently been pestering him with tales of a satanic gerbil, making him reluctant to answer its screeching.

"Mrs. Marigold, how can I help?"

"Is that Harold Sinker?" asked a male voice.

"Yes, to whom am I speaking?"

"I am an old friend of Mr. Sudsy. I would like to know how you are getting on with his evaluation?"

Leaning forward, Harold went to rest his whisky glass on the desk's leather carapace, saying, "Sorry, but I am not at liberty to discuss that. Patient-client confidentiality, you know. Besides, the court case is pending, would you li…"

The calm voice interjected, "I'm sure you'll do a great job. In fact, I think you'll find that Mr. Sudsy has a mental condition that will absolve him of all responsibility."

Harold's single malt began to lap against the walls of the crystal glass as his hand shook.

"Did you think your shitty little practice got this case by accident?" continued the voice, this time with a slightly gruffer edge. "Oh no! Mr. Sudsy made sure that his evaluation came to you - his wimpy ex-classmate. You are going to help us out, Harold. You know it, and so do I. Remember how you were always the last pick at football – well, things haven't changed."

"Wait a min…," but the phone line had gone dead.

Harold sat in silence for several seconds before gulping down his nightcap. Then, reaching across, he plucked the case file from his attaché case.

Shaking his head, he thought, *'Maybe the call was a hoax: maybe from one of his old classmates who had seen the court listing in the Grimsby Herald.'*

He galloped through the case file until he reached a gory anecdote on page 52.

'Although Mr Sudsy is predominantly a charmer and womaniser - he must have kissed the Blarney Stone whilst still in nappies as he has a predisposition for violence which can flare up at a moment's notice. During a Soap Suds sales conference in Cleethorpes, he bludgeoned an employee with a three-litre carton of detergent after catching him texting during a presentation. He went berserk and, using any implement within reach as a cudgel, he repeatedly whacked the man with a toilet brush, mop, and some sanitary towels. I will never forget the pink effervescence, as the blood mixed with the soap powder on the boardroom floor. That day, he made Caligula look like Bill Oddie.'

Testament of Tony Furk, Soap Suds Managing Director.'

A further brief pillage of the case file revealed more violence and skirmishes. There were also some dalliances with the Yorkshire underworld, plus a slew of unpaid alimonies. It appears the glare of the police had been on Mr. Sudsy for quite some time. However, having some, supposedly, heavyweight political connections they had been kept at bay. Mr Sudsy wasn't just a rich farceur (*); he was a rich, violent farceur. Whilst there had always been a hint of a fly undone, now he was wielding a tyre iron in his right hand.

Harold yanked open the bureau drawer and quickly grasped for his vial of valium.

* * * * *

Over the next fortnight, Harold began to re-read Lolita. During a torpid Sunday lunch with his wife (in which the kids had promised to come, but once again had cancelled at the eleventh-hour,) he had begun to ponder on Vladimir Nabokov's inspiration for the novel. He had been moved by a newspaper article - probably having been in some émigré broadsheet - that told of an ape who had been raised in captivity and had been taught to communicate and perform human tasks. When the ape was given a sheet of paper and a set of crayons, it had sketched the bars of its cage. On reading how Nabokov described the incident, Harold felt such empathy with the primate that he nearly burst into tears.

However, his pity was tempered by his own reticence, so he only managed a dignified sniffle.

"Harold, would you like some more gravy?" his wife asked from the stern of the dining table.

Harold gaped at the faded certificates and photos that peppered the walls. Now his two daughters had left home all that remained was the detritus (*) of what had always been a flimsy marriage.

"Harold! Would you like some gravy?"

"No, I'm fine," he muttered, ushering some peas around his plate.

The ape lingered in Harold's brain; it wouldn't relent. And he pictured himself drawing on a sheet of manila - sketching his iron bed frame, with a set of L-plates on the headboard.

"Good, Mr. Ape Man," said the white-coated operative. "Now, put the banana in the slot."

Harold wrested the keys from the imaginary zookeeper before bounding out the door.

"Harold! Where are you going?" yelled his wife.

"The study! I need to phone Mr. Sudsy."

* * * * *

(*)waste material or rubbish   18

The night before the trial arrived with the air of a doctor's waiting room. Harold was lying in bed with the case file strewn over his ill-fitting pyjamas. His right eyebrow twitched at will, and two generous sweat patches adorned his oxters (*).

He washed down a handful of diazepam with some tepid hot chocolate. The tension of the preceding weeks had induced vomiting, weight loss, and chronic masturbation. He extended each of his fingers in sequence, trying in vain to tot up how many opiates he had taken that day.

Finally, regaining some sangfroid, he peered down at the case file. A final skim would ensure that there were no holes in his testimony. Despite the imminent risk of death or imprisonment he was, in some perverse way, actually starting to relish 'The Adventures of Mr. Sudsy.' It had all the reckless drama of the Old Testament.

He thumbed to the lewdness, on page 72.

'Sudsy would regularly hold orgies in his Alcázar in Scunthorpe. Everybody would attend: the local police commissioner, mayor, minor politicians, Russ Abbot - all of society's casualties.

At one party, he waltzed in naked, wearing just cricket pads and brandishing a King Eddie cigar. He got everyone to slather themselves in baby oil and play Twister in the buff. No expense was spared, once hiring Black Lace to play in the conservatory. I distinctly remember Mr. Sudsy getting a reach around from a Maggie Philbin lookalike.'

Testament of Tom Tunt, Mr. Sudsy's Chauffeur.

Harold looked over at his pallid wife. He saw the tight perm that vibrated with every passing snore, and the washed-out nightie that hung off her shoulders like a Marks & Spencer's pall.

In his twenties, he had had a wild fling with a Jamaican hussy at Hull University. He had wanted to marry her but society, and his parents, had disapproved.

Instead, he had settled for a Caucasian wallflower. He glared down at his wife's thin lips, wondering if he should leave her behind tomorrow. Sighing, he rolled onto his side and quietly masturbated, eventually reaching a meek climax somewhere off the Caribbean coast.

* * * * *

The gentle shunt of the train lulled Harold into a state of childish bliss. Outside, the green countryside flashed by unannounced.

Suddenly, his mobile phone began to vibrate. Harold tried to ignore it, but he wondered if it was the police – perhaps they had caught up with him.

Swiping up the phone from the seat, he squinted at the text message and sighed then started to tap a reply, but the words wouldn't flow. Since he had turned forty-five, the latency between his thoughts and fumbling prose had steadily grown. Eventually, he ditched the fancy Latin and went for the jugular.

'Mrs. Marigold, Harry Secombe died some time ago. In any case, he did not wear leather chaps and certainly did not waggle a purple dildo. Please take two valium and go straight to bed. I am going on a long holiday. Please contact Dr. Tartae in my absence.'

* * * * *

The carriage door clattered open, causing Harold to flinch. It was the train conductor - a tall man with a fat, inviting face. Harold fished the tickets out of his suit trousers, surrendering them with a nervous smile. The man inspected the tickets and quickly handed them back.

"Merci, Monsieur Sudsy."

Harold chuckled as the man retreated into the

passageway. He sank back into his seat and closed his eyes. He was glad his little ruse had worked. His false testimony had persuaded the jury to acquit Mr Sudsy on the grounds of mental illness.

Harold fondled the leather briefcase on his lap. It was crammed with the money he had extorted from Mr. Sudsy so that he would lie in court.

However, later that day, his anonymous phone call to the police revealed that Mr Sudsy was an old classmate of his, making his testimony void and thus triggering a retrial.

At this juncture Harold was already 500 miles south of Hull. For the first time in years, Harold felt a gentle throb in his undercarriage and a nubile flutter in his chest – similar to the first pangs of adolescence.

The carriage door clattered open again. Harold spun around. It was his wife, clutching an Eccles cake and a plastic cup of tea. She zig-zagged across the carriage before lurching onto the seat beside him.

"I thought the Eurostar was meant to be smooth?" she protested, perching the cake on top of her Dick Francis novel, before slurping her milky tea.

"Harold dear, does it rain much in Antibes? I forgot to pack my light jacket," she inquired, nibbling the perimeter of her cake.

"No, Vera, I don't think it rains much at all. I do believe the weather is going to be just fine."

© *Stephen Pollock*

Images licensed to Pen & Ink Designs Publishing

LUCKY IN LOVE

'You'll be the only cock in the henhouse!'

This was scribbled on the bottom of Michael's invitation. There was no mistaking Gina's handwriting. It was so illegible that she should have been a doctor.

He binned the envelope and stuck the bubble-gum-coloured card on the fridge with blu-tack. It was in two weeks' time, but he'd known about it for months. The countdown to Gina's hen night had been as long in the planning as the Second Coming. She'd been talking about it for years. Wanting everything to be perfect. And Michael, as best friend of the bride-to-be, had been privy to every minute detail of the itinerary.

In the initial stages, he'd assumed he would have been able to escape the hen weekend for gender reasons. Michael was hardly a traditionalist, but he figured that being a man would pretty much exclude him from the activities. And even though he'd vainly attempted to excuse himself the previous week, she had made it quite clear over the phone that his attendance was mandatory.

"You're not being let off the hook, sweetheart. I need you there, every step of the way. Somebody's got to be there to check that I don't make a complete tit of myself. I'll probably end up bladdered and cop off with someone, meaning the pictures will end up on Facebook the next day.

Rob will then call the whole thing off, and I'll have to spend the next ten years paying off the credit card bills. The dress alone has cost a fortune. You know what the girls at work are like."

"Yes, but they're hardly going to spike your drinks with Rohypnol. And calling them 'girls' is being rather charitable, isn't it? Most of them aren't really in the first bloom of youth," he had responded. But still to no avail.

At the end of the conversation, he had put the receiver down, knowing that no excuse would be good enough to secure his absence. Although not a religious man, he prayed for an Act of God.

And now, there was no turning back. It was official. He had the invitation to prove it.

* * * * *

Michael was meeting Gina for a coffee that

Saturday afternoon and knew what the topic of conversation would be.

When she arrived, laden with shopping bags, he stood up to kiss her.

"I didn't think your wardrobes could hold any more clothes?" he said.

"I had a big clear-out last night," she told him as she sat down.

"That doesn't mean you've got to replace them all straight away."

"Oh, stop being such an old nag and get me a latte. I'm parched."

No sooner had Michael returned with her drink than Gina took a sip and then started on her favourite topic of conversation.

'So, what are you going to wear? You know it's got to be pink, don't you?'

"I was hoping that I might get a special dispensation as I'm the only bloke," he pleaded.

"No exceptions. Besides, I thought that was your signature colour."

"Just because I'm gay, doesn't mean I have a

plethora of pink attire."

She laughed. "Get you and your posh words. We went to the same school, remember? I knew you when you struggled to spell 'cat.' Anyway, you haven't answered my question, what are you going to wear? Why don't you drag up? Everyone would love it."

"Except for me. You know I wouldn't do that sort of thing. I've bought a new pastel pink polo shirt. I was going to wear that."

"Hardly pushing the boat out, are you?" she gasped.

"Well, I didn't want to eclipse you on your big night. So, what's it to be for you – Lurex boob tube and a thong?"

"I'll have you know that now I'm approaching my thirtieth birthday, I am dressing in a more demur fashion."

Michael struggled to keep his gulp of hot chocolate inside his mouth. After he had swallowed it, he replied, "Pardon me, while I take all that in. So… you're renouncing your old slapper ways."

"I'm just learning to act my age, that's all. I

thought you'd be proud of me. Besides, I've got Rob to think of, that's all. When are **you** going to find somebody to settle down with?"

Michael shook his head, "Let's not go there today. We both know I'm simply not the marrying kind. Let's talk about you."

They both felt more comfortable with that choice of subject matter.

Eventually, Gina continued with, "Anway, it doesn't mean I can't have one last bender, pardon the expression, on my hen night." And as she said this, she pulled out a folded piece of paper from her handbag and handed it to Michael. "This is the updated itinerary for next Saturday."

"This must be your tenth version, at least," he said as he glanced at the times and instructions.

"Well, I just want it to be perfect."

"Mmm..." was his only response.

* * * * *

The day of the hen night arrived.

Michael felt it was petty to point out that, technically, it was a hen day and night as the first event began at eight-thirty in the morning. That was a champagne breakfast at a seafront hotel. He was glad that there was an opportunity for a disco nap for a couple of hours. But that wasn't until five o'clock. Until then, he had nine and a half hours of fish pedicure, rollercoasters on the pier, a pamper session at a spa, ten-pin bowling, and a cream tea. Then and only then could he get a few hours of respite.

His best friend had extremely eclectic tastes. Fortunately, Gina had followed his advice which meant that serious alcohol consumption would not be starting until the evening.

As it turned out, Michael enjoyed the day, ensuring he kept checking on his best friend.

"Are you enjoying yourself, Gee?"

"You bet. Those fish tickled my feet. Do you think they do any good? You should have had a go."

"No way," he replied in horror. "I wasn't going to dip my tootsies in there. God knows how many verrucas have been in there. I feel sorry for the poor fish. Not much of a life, is it?"

"Don't get all animal rights on me. I want today to be perfect," said Gina.

"I'm glad you're having a good time, Gee. But, I just wanted to ask if I could duck out of the early evening bingo session you have planned…?"

Gina didn't even allow him to finish the sentence.

"You, young man, are going to be with me every step of the way. We're booked in for the early bird special at six o'clock. Then the minibus is going to take us to the restaurant at eight before we go clubbing until the wee small hours of the morning. Who knows what might happen? You might even crack a smile."

"But do I really have to come along to the bingo? I could pop back and meet up with you all at the pizza place."

She gave him one of her withering looks and arched her eyebrows.

There was a slight pause, before Michael continued. "I'll take that as a 'No' then."

"Thank you, Michael. After all, this is my big day, **and** I want everything to go just as I have planned it."

Good manners prevented him from saying that

the wedding would really be her big day, but he knew better than to contradict her.

"Well, let me sit next to you so you can show me what to do. You know I get all mixed up with numbers."

"It's a deal, and if you're a good boy, I'll buy you a really thick felt tip pen for crossing off the numbers."

* * * * *

Later, at the bingo hall, Gina let slip that Michael had never been before. This prompted a couple of Gina's work colleagues to name him their little virgin. Their cackling laughter would not have been out of place in The Scottish Play. They told him that everybody has to have a first time and that there was nothing to be scared of.

Despite Gina's refusals, Michael bought the first round of drinks.

'Lighten up, Gee, it's the evening. We've done pretty well so far. It'll get us all in the mood. Plus, I'm going to need this."

"You're such a drama queen, Michael. I'm not sending you in front of a firing squad. You're just having a game of bingo. You might even enjoy it."

Taking hold of his hand, Gina led him to one of the booths that she had reserved for them all. And true to her word, she sat him next to her.

Next, she handed him a pack of different coloured papers that were stapled together into a booklet before explaining what he had to do. Michael was shocked to see that some of her friends had more than one booklet.

"How on Earth can they check more than one set of numbers?" he asked fearfully.

Gina patted his hand. "They're old hands at this. My Mum can manage four at a time, but we are going to start you off gently."

There was no disguising the fact that Gina's

entourage was a hen party. The fact that all twenty of them were dressed in pink might also have been a bit of a give-away.

A member of staff approached Michael to ask for the bride-to-be's name.

A few minutes later, the bingo caller tapped the microphone to test it was on, then he welcomed everyone to the first session of the evening. There was a muted cheer, so he pretended he couldn't hear.

Gina was the loudest to cheer. "He's a bit of all right, isn't he, Mikey?"

"I suppose so, but don't forget that you're a soon-to-be-married woman."

"Spoilsport!" And she grinned at him.

The caller laughed and continued, "Good evening, ladies and…." He scanned the room, then continued, "Ah yes, and gentleman! I see there's one brave man who's ventured out with the hen party this evening. Let's give Gina and her crew a big hand."

After the applause had subsided, he went on.

"My name's Andy, and my job is to make sure that each and every one of you have a great evening. So, eyes down for the first card of the evening. Be lucky." And he gave a cheesy grin as he winked in Gina's direction.

"Did you see that, Mikey? He's trying it on with me. My luck's in."

One of Gina's friends shouted across that he might fix the numbers for her, so she'd win or, at the very least, get them a round of free drinks.

Michael didn't appreciate the attention they were receiving, particularly because some of her friends were speaking loudly, and even shouting. And that was before they'd had lots to drink. *'It was going to be a long night,'* he thought.

It took all of Michael's concentration to keep up with the numbers being called out. He was surprised at how exciting he found it. He only had two numbers to go before he heard a woman screech out from the other side of the hall, "House!"

Gina glanced at the first page of his bingo booklet. "You were so close, Mikey. You only needed two more. It must be beginner's luck. Better luck with the next one. It's just about to start."

He just had time to take a swig of his gin and tonic before Andy began calling out the numbers. This time, Michael was even closer to winning. He was just waiting for number eight to be called out.

He couldn't believe his misfortune when Andy announced number eighteen, and one of the hen party stood up to claim her prize. He feigned enthusiasm but felt robbed. He didn't even know what the prize money was, he just wanted to win.

As the third game started, Gina started telling

him a story about one of the women from work. After ignoring her for a minute or two, he turned and shushed her, added, 'I'm trying to concentrate.'

"Get you! This is hardly rocket science." She reached across for his bingo booklet, but he quickly snatched it back.

"Damn, I missed the last number. Look what you've made me do."

"Keep your hair on, Mikey. They show them up on the screen." And she pointed to the plasma screen behind Andy's head.

Michael didn't do so well that time. He was six numbers away, feeling his luck was deserting him.

There were a few more games, and then Andy announced a short interval - a time to refresh their drinks – but promising to return in twenty minutes with some games with even bigger prizes. Then jumping off the stage he walked in the direction of the hen party.

One of her friends nudged her, saying, "He's coming our way, Gina."

She quickly turned to Michael. "Have I got lipstick on my teeth?"

"No, you're OK."

"How about my hair?" she asked.

"Fabulous, although you're wearing enough hairspray that a medium-sized hurricane would struggle to make an impact on it."

Andy introduced himself to the group, and Gina's friends huddled around her.

"So, Gina, this is rather unconventional."

"What do you mean, Andy?" she asked, flashing her very best smile and hundreds of pounds of dental veneers.

"Well, isn't it customary to spend your hen night with just your female friends and leave your fiancé at home?"

This caused a lot of laughter from everyone with the exception of Michael. He couldn't quite see what was so funny about the misunderstanding.

"Michael... my fiancé? No, he's my oldest friend in the whole wide world. And, as he never tires of telling me, he's not the marrying kind. If you catch my drift, Andy. He's here to make sure I don't get into any trouble this evening from predatory males."

Michael couldn't be sure, but he was pretty certain that Gina had winked as she'd said that.

"So, where are you all heading off to later?"

Gina spelled out the name of the nightclub they were going to.

Andy nodded, saying, "Maybe I'll see you, ladies, then. I'll send a member of the bar staff across to provide you all with some complimentary drinks. To get you in the mood for later."

Then, smiling, he left them to return to the stage.

By the time the second round of bingo games was due to start, Gina had a row of drinks lined up in front of her on the table.

As Andy read out the numbers, she whispered to Michael often, "Can you see Andy looking across at me all the time? He's not very subtle, is he?"

"You're loving every minute of it, Gina. Just enjoy the attention and the flattery but don't you dare do anything to screw up your relationship with Rob. I forked out a lot on your wedding present."

"Don't worry about me, Mikey. I've had plenty worse than Andy, and of course, I'm flattered. But now Rob's put this ring on my finger, I'm spoken for.

I'll let him down gently, and if he's persistent, I'll get Janet to go after him. She's a man-eater, that one. We call her the Mountie because she always gets her man. That way, he won't go home disappointed, and my conscience will be intact."

Michael was keen for them to get to the restaurant, as Gina had been drinking on an empty stomach and was now slightly slurring her words.

As they put their coats on, Andy came up to them again. "So where are you all off to now? It's a bit early for a nightclub. Although, since none of you were big bingo winners this evening, maybe you'll be luckier in love."

"Pass the sick bucket, will you?" Michael stage-whispered to Gina, and she elbowed him in the ribs.

"Well, I know I am, Andy." She emphasised the fact by waving her left hand in front of his face so that he could get a good look at her diamond engagement ring.

Andy stood with them while they waited for their minibus to pick them up. After a few minutes of small talk, Gina decided to spell it out to Andy.

"Listen, Andy, you're a good-looking bloke, and you seem friendly, but I'm just not interested. Perhaps a few years ago I would have…."

He interrupted her, "I think you've got the wrong end of the stick, Gina."

She smiled. "I don't think so, Mate. I've been around the block a few times myself and you don't think I can't recognise the signs when a guy's coming on to me? If you do come along to the club later, I just want to make it crystal clear to you that I'm not available, although there are plenty of other women in my hen party who might be interested."

Andy cleared his throat, looked away then back at Gina. "It is one of your friends I am keen to get to know better. It's just that I never found out his name!" And he smiled to take the sting out of the comment.

* * * * *

Gina and Rob had glorious weather for their wedding day. It all went perfectly as planned. And as it happened, there was no gap in the seating plan, for Michael had found somebody to be his 'plus one' at the top table. Guess who?

© *Andrew Kearsey*

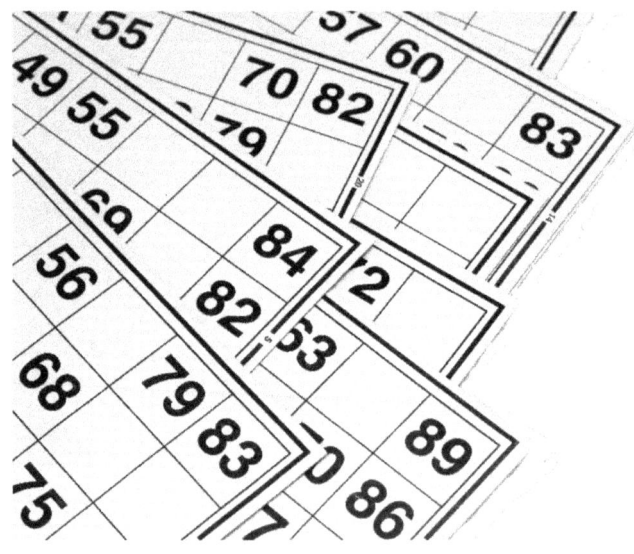

Images licensed to Pen & Ink Designs Publishing

THE GOODBYE

Chessy considered herself to be in prison whilst in the rehab facility. Not because of the rules, but as a result of an accident. A fall that had resulted in her left knee being smashed into twenty pieces and her femur being broken.

Five hours of surgery had fixed her knee and femur; and now, after what had seemed 'like ages,' she was waiting impatiently for her husband, Bryan, to arrive to take her home.

She was sat in a large club chair in the open-area on the sixth floor of the Village Rehabilitation Center. The possessions she had accumulated whilst there were on either side of the chair, and her walker was in front of her, within easy reach.

Although she was sure Bryan had told her he wouldn't be there until between two and two-thirty, she knew she had to be out of her room by ten-thirty. It was one of the facility's rules. As such, she was left sitting in the club chair for several hours.

During the wait, she spent part of the time re-reading 'The Maltese Falcon' and part of the time thinking or remembering how the accident had happened. She also thought about her other accident, when she had fractured her hip, also on her left side.

As the day passed, she sat there through lunchtime. The tables in the area were being used by the residents to eat their lunch. They were also utilised the same way for breakfast and dinner.

Rethinking about how each of her accidents occurred, she recalled they had been in different places and under different circumstances.

When she fell and fractured her hip, she had been walking on Park Row, across from City Hall Park. From the way she described it to Bryan and herself immediately after it happened, it was that her left side had felt as if it had just given way. She attributed that feeling and the resulting fall to her osteoporosis.

But her more recent accident had a much different scenario. The first accident had left her walking with a cane; often leaving her feeling unsteady on her feet. A normally petite woman, she had lost several inches as a result of having osteoporosis and was smaller than when she had fractured her hip.

This time, the accident occurred in front of The Museum of Jewish Heritage. She had been waiting for a bus to take her to the Seaport. From there, she had planned on walking a block up Fulton Street to the market to buy some Soy Pudding.

Three buses had passed her by. Determined to stop the next bus, she had left the bench, stepped into the gutter, and leaned on a parked car. Moments later, the car had pulled away, and down she went. That was the beginning of her ordeal, although it would be over in a matter of hours.

Since it was close to lunchtime, residents who were capable of eating at a table began to arrive. Most of them were in their seventies or, like her, their eighties. They navigated with the aid of their canes, wheelchairs, or walkers, similar to what Chessy used. She would continue to use a walker until her injured knee and femur healed enough for her to use a cane again.

Never a foodie, she detested institutional food, depending on Bryan to bring her sandwiches from the outside or, even better, to take her to one of the nearby restaurants in a wheelchair. Getting out of the facility was more important to her than the food she'd ordered.

Although billed as a rehab facility, it was, according to her, also a holding pen for individuals who needed long-term care. Or those who were close to dying and needed to remain in their rooms until they passed. However, some of the long-term residents made it to the tables without help or were brought to them in wheelchairs by the nurse's aides. It was a sad parade that she had so far not witnessed because it depressed her.

But this time, there was no way for her to avoid it as she had the best seat 'in the house.' From it, she could see all the tables and the people seated at them. It was as if she was experiencing a 'luncheon show' that had been organized for her benefit.

She wondered if the people at the various tables knew that she was going home. Surely, the bags of clothing and the valise near her were a giveaway, a clear indication that she would be leaving.

Not the type to ruminate on the subject, the focus of her whole being was on the time Bryan would arrive and take her away from the place that she had dubbed 'The prison.'

Oh, she had made a few friends here, but she shunned those who wanted to be her friends, holding herself aloof from them.

Time passed slowly, but by the end of the day, Bryan still hadn't come. Sadly, she returned to her room, convinced she had somehow gotten the wrong day again and that he would come tomorrow. She didn't tell anyone that Bryan hadn't come for her.

The next day she repeated the same actions. As far as she was concerned, the big clock on the wall of her room behind her bed was meaningless. Its hands moved, but their movement had nothing to do with her.

Eventually, her hair turned grey, and her body withered to that belonging to an old lady, belying the beautiful woman she had once been.

If she spoke to anyone, she spoke to herself so that no one could hear her. It was almost always a one-sided conversation in which she did all of the talking, although now and then, there were other voices. Those of her mother, her father, Bryan, and Bill, a music teacher she had known long ago. But when these voices came, they were always very faint and were growing fainter each day until she could barely hear them.

Sometimes, she remembered events, family dinners, going to Venice with Bryan, and even playing the piano. When she thought about that, she always exclaimed to herself, "Imagine that!"

It was something she couldn't believe. So, she would ruefully say, "All gone now."

It was that afternoon when the three women at the table not far from where she sat waiting for Bryan turned to her. Two were white, and one was black.

The three, who were incredibly old, had to be spoon-fed by a staff member. They, too, spoke to no one. The Black lady wore a man's grey hat, but her head was flopped to one side.

The other two constantly stared at the ceiling. Today, the three of them were looking at her, something that had never happened before.

The Black lady said, "Today, he will come. Goodbye."

Then the other two said, "Goodbye" in unison.

Chessy happily answered, "Goodbye."

Each of them smiled at her, and there he was, coming toward her. At that moment, she felt a cold darkness enveloping her, and then she didn't feel anything.

Only Bryan was there, holding her hand.

© *Irving A Greenfield*

Images licensed to Pen & Ink Designs Publishing

YOU ARE MY SUNSHINE

Twenty-seven-year-old Jared James is waiting alone in the practically empty pub. A regular gets angry at the fruit machine, while a pretty waitress wipes down tables as the barfly reads his newspaper.

You could say Jared's handsome, but not leading-man handsome! More the guy who pines for the girl next door than the one who has ladies lining up around the block. He toys with a tiny jewellery box; big enough to hold an engagement ring.

A girl enters, catching her sleeve on the door but not seeing the funny side. Jared swiftly pockets the jewellery box. The girl frees her jacket sleeve and stomps over.

Jared rises like a gentleman, saying, "Hey, Tiffany."

He moves in for a greeting kiss, but all he gets is a sharp peck on the cheek. He pulls a chair out for his special lady, only to get a tetchy, "I can do it!" growl.

"Bloody, car parks. They've put the price up again!" moans Tiffany. "I didn't have enough change, so I had to park all the way out of town."

The waitress eavesdrops on Tiffany's rant. She catches Jared's gaze, and they exchange a brief innocent smile… which Tiffany clocks.

"What the hell was that?" sneers Tiffany.

"What was what?" Jared asks innocently.

"You know what!"

Jared looks at the waitress, but she retreats to the bar.

"Am I interrupting your date?" says Tiffany through gritted teeth.

"Tiffany, come on, what's with you today?" he asks, reaching out to hold her hand.

She pulls her hand back and takes a calming breath. "Look, Jared. I'm sorry. It's just not working out. I don't feel the same way about you anymore."

"What because of that?"

"No, it's …"

"I look at another woman for a split second, and

you want to throw two years away!"

"It's got nothing to do with that. Listen, we both know it's not been right for a while now. We just... don't have anything in common. I think we're just too different."

Jared slumps back in his chair; the wind taken out of his sails.

"I'll go to my mother's tonight," she exclaims standing up. "I'll get my stuff from the flat tomorrow while you're at work. I'm sorry, Jared."

As Tiffany heads to the exit, Jared opens the Jewellery box. There's no ring inside. Instead, a tiny ballerina figurine starts to dance to the tune - *'You Are My Sunshine.'*

Tiffany stops still. Confusion washes over her. She blinks twice, swivels around, and seeing Jared her face lights up. She's suddenly giddied with excitement.

"There's my handsome boy!" she announces with elation.

Tiffany skips over and throws her arms around Jared, before planting a big kiss on his lips.

The Pub regular and the barfly watch on bewildered. Even the waitress is not sure what to make of the tongue wrestling.

Finally, Tiffany releases herself from the embrace and asks if he's missed her.

"As always," smiles Jared. "You wanna order some food?"

Tiffany looks Jared up and down like a lion hunting a gazelle. She nibbles her lip and flashes a look with her mischievous eyes.

"How about we skip mains and go straight to dessert?" she proposes.

And before Jared has a chance to speak, Tiffany grabs his collar and leads him out the door, almost colliding with a girl handing out yellow flyers.

The next morning, Jared lies on the bed covers, with the weight of the world on his mind. A calendar on the wall has February 14th circled in red pen.

Tiffany appears. She crawls on top of him in her underwear and snuggles close. "I wish I could stay in bed with you all day!" she says.

"Then stay in bed with me all day," Jared replies.

"I can't. I have to go to work."

She starts to move away, only for Jared to gently usher her back for another kiss. She doesn't take much persuasion.

"You're such a bad influence on me!" Tiffany pouts as she gives him one more sensual kiss then pulls herself away.

"I have to go," says Tiffany. "I'll be back before you know it."

Tiffany slips into her Nurse's uniform.

"You better be," says Jared.

"And, if you're particularly good, maybe I'll wear the 'other' nurse's outfit for you later."

Jared grins like a Cheshire cat.

Tiffany laughs. She leans over for a goodbye kiss and says, 'Love you."

"Love you more!" replies Jared.

Tiffany prances off to work as Jared goes to the bathroom to brush his teeth. He catches his reflection in the mirror and can't help but stare.

DING DONG... The doorbell chimes.

Ambling into the hallway, Jared opens the front door.

On the other side is the waitress from the bar wearing a familiar frown.

"Don't give me that look!" he says.

Jared saunters into the kitchen, followed by the waitress, otherwise known as Aubrey.

"How many times is that?" she asks. "Seven?"

"Actually, it's eight," he says.

"When are you going to admit defeat? Double figures!"

"I'll definitely review it when it's approaching treble."

Aubrey shakes her head in mock dismay. She opens the fridge and helps herself to a crumpet. Then she rummages inside the top cupboard and pulls out a jar of jam.

"Please, make yourself at home," says Jared.

Aubrey giggles, grabs a knife, scoops the last of the jam from the jar onto her cold crumpet, and then haphazardly tosses the knife in the sink, much to Jared's annoyance.

"You're a bit tetchy for someone who got laid last night," she remarks. "Should I presume that is guilt you are feeling!"

Something suddenly catches her eye.

She holds up a silver necklace with a heart-shaped locket, asking, 'Is this Tiffany's?'

Jared scurries over, swiping the necklace from her grasp before she can open the locket. "That's nothing!" he exclaims.

Aubrey sidesteps away with her crumpet, jokingly putting her hands up in surrender as he stashes the locket at the back of a drawer.

She gazes at an old-fashioned hypnosis stage show poster up on the wall. The headline act reads 'The Great Rhamantus'.

"Was that your dad?" she enquires.

"Yeah, that's him."

"I'm guessing he taught you."

"Before he retired."

Did your dad ever hypnotize your mum to keep the love alive, or did you come-up with that trick all by yourself?

"I'll ignore that remark!"

Aubrey smirks, takes a bite of the crumpet, and pulls a face of revulsion.

"Urgh, how old was that Jam?" she moans.

"To be honest, I didn't know we had any," he smirks.

"Neither Tiff nor I like it, so it could've been there for years."

Aubrey wipes her tongue and dry gags.

"Don't be such a drama queen," he teases. "Come on, I'll buy you a hot chocolate to get rid of the taste."

"Yeah, I bet that's what you tell all the girls."

* * * * *

Half an hour later, they're sipping hot chocolate milk in a tiny family-run café.

"So," Aubrey begins, "Does Tiffany fall head over heels every time she hears that song and rushes home to seduce you?"

"It's only when it's played on this!" says Jared

placing the musical jewellery box on the table. "It has a unique pitch," he adds.

"Aren't there loads of these toys?"

"Not like this. I made it myself. Some hypnotists use a universal sound or a keyword as a trigger, but it's harder to control."

"And you can get people to do anything?" asks Aubrey.

"Depends how susceptible to the suggestion they are, but yeah, you can get them to act a certain way or even forget complete chunks of their lives. Sky's the limit."

"So, the one that got away is here to stay!"

"Tiffany isn't the one who got away."

"No."

"Before Tiffany, I was with this other girl. We met in high school and dated all through college and university," he explains.

"Jeez, what did the count reach with her?"

"I never hypnotized her. I wasn't hedging my bets back then."

"So, what happened?" Aubrey asks.

"I guess… I took her for granted. As the years went by, I got wrapped up in law school. And she had her own dreams to follow. Our relationship took second place. Then suddenly, the magic was gone. It's only when you say goodbye to someone you realize how much you miss them. We tried to get back together a few times after the split, but it was never the same. It felt forced. Wasn't natural anymore. Whatever we had, was lost. She no longer looked at me the way she used to anymore. Too many bad memories to cloud over the good ones."

"Is she the girl in the locket?" Aubrey asks.

Jared nods and sighs. "What I'd give to have just one final hour together like it was at the beginning. When it was pure. When she loved me. I know it's not meant to be, but that doesn't stop me wanting one last dance, you know. All I want is to see her look at me like she used to, one last time, and mean it, then I could let go."

Aubrey feels for Jared as he stirs his drink and stares out the window.

Barely a week later, Jared returns from work to find Tiffany sitting on the couch beside packed boxes and a suitcase. Her demeanour is solemn, and her voice soft as she asks him to sit beside her. He questions why, yet knowing exactly what's coming.

"I'm sorry, Jared," she says. "I've tried, but something just doesn't feel right. I think we've both been thinking about it."

Then she rises and takes hold of her suitcase.

"You'll make someone really happy one day!" she says. "I'm just sorry it wasn't me."

Tiffany offers a consoling smile, and with a gentle squeeze on his arm, she wheels her suitcase towards the hallway.

Jared removes the Musical Jewellery box from his pocket... but hesitates before opening the case.

As Tiffany places her house keys on a side cabinet she glances back, saying, "Take care of yourself, Jared."

As she walks down the hallway to the front door, Jared's fingers are still poised on the lid. He stares long and hard at the jewellery box... then finally, he takes his fingers away. He hears the front door click shut and Tiffany is gone.

Later that night, as Jarod sits perched on a bar

stool, the local bartender pours him another Jagerbomb. Suddenly, Aubrey emerges from a backroom staircase with an overflowing laundry bag. She spots her friend looking the worse for wear so lugs the washing bag over.

"You let her go?" she asks him.

Jared nods. His eyes are heavy as he's been drinking for hours.

"It might not feel like it now," she adds, "but you did the right thing."

Jared swirls the drink around.

Aubrey spots a yellow flyer on a nearby table. She places it in front of Jared and can't help but smirk.

"Fancy it?" She asks.

Jared squints to focus his blurred vision. The flyer reads: 'An evening of Hypnosis with Miss Leondra Mystique.'

Jared screws the flyer into a ball and shoves it in his gob. He starts to munch.

"A simple no would have sufficed!" Aubrey giggles.

Jared spits out the soggy, mushed-up paper.

"Living here now, are you?" he asks, referring to the dirty clothes.

"Until a rich husband materializes to rescue me!"

Jared surveys the surroundings, empty except for a couple of downtrodden old men drowning their sorrows.

"Good luck with that!" says Jared as he picks up his drink.

"You know Jägermeister used to be made from deer's blood... that's why there's a deer on the bottle."

"To the dearly departed," he toasts.

Aubrey rolls her eyes as Jared necks the drink in one. He grimaces at the strength, then gestures to the bartender for a refill.

"That's not the answer!" states Aubrey.

"You've not heard the question," Jared replies as the bartender fixes him another.

"Come on, let's get out of here. I need to eat."

"Get something here."

Jared swaps money for the booze. As he motions to down it, Aubrey sticks her thumb in his way.

"What am I supposed to do with that?" he says.

"Let's have a thumb war," suggests Aubrey. "You win, and I'll buy us Jagerbombs all night, and you can drink yourself into a hospital bed. I win; you come do laundry with me, and then your buy me chips."

"You want a thumb war... exactly how old are you?"

"Free drinks all night!"

Jared puts his glass down and they lock hands.

"Start the countdown."

"One, two, three, four... I declare a thumb war."

Jared jousts for position but can't tangle Aubrey's thumb. He gets it for a split second but Aubrey wriggles clear.

"You'll never win this!" he says.

"Go on, pin me then."

Jared and Aubrey persevere with the thumb war. Finally, Aubrey clocks something behind Jared, and her smile fades.

"Oh no," she says. "Tiffany has just walked in."

Jared looks around... Aubrey hooks his thumb into a pin. There's no sign of Tiffany.

"Yes!" Aubrey gloats. "One, two, three... we have ourselves a winner."

"You're such a cheat."

"A win's a win, my friend. This way, loser."

Jared gets up to leave. He takes hold of his drink, but Aubrey snatches the glass and downs it. Jared is impressed.

Aubrey turns green. "Yuck... I shouldn't have done that!"

Not long after, Jared found he had swapped staring into the bottom of a glass for gawking at clothes going round and round in a tumble dryer.

"Won't make them dry any faster," says Aubrey. "Hey, you know why unmanned launderettes have these harsh neon blue lights on at night? Its so junkies can't see the veins to shoot up. Public toilets use the same bulbs."

"Well, aren't you full of fun facts tonight!" he replies.

"I try... you still have the.... you know what?"

Jared plays dumb but isn't fooling anyone. He sighs and pulls the musical jewellery box from his pocket.

"Still clinging onto a lifeline, eh!" says Aubrey. "You know what has to be done. I'll leave you two alone."

Aubrey goes over to stop the machine and shuffles her laundry back into the bag.

Jared opens the jewellery box. He watches the ballerina figurine dance to the *'You are my Sunshine'* tune.

Slowly, he places it on the tiled floor and raises his foot over the top. Then, contemplating for a moment, he takes a breath, and with a heavy heart... he stomps it into a dozen pieces.

"Feel better?" asks Aubrey.

Jared raises his eyeline. A smile blossoms. Aubrey is wearing a bra over her head like earmuffs. She looks over her shoulder as though there is something funny on the wall behind her. Jared can't help but grin.

"There's that famous smile!" she teases. "Come on, you owe me chips."

Slowly, the pair stroll along the cobbled moonlit streets as Aubrey munches away on newspaper-wrapped chips. She holds one out for Jared to take a bite, then shoves it in her gob at the last minute.

He playfully goes for the chips. But she giggles and shields them with her body. He wraps his arms around her waist, and she spins around into his embrace.

Words are forgotten as their eyes do the talking. They gaze into each other's pupils, as if they were the only two people on the planet. Within minutes the pair have burst through Jared's front door and piled into the wall. Kissing passionately, they are lost in the moment.

Parting lips for a split second for Aubrey to peel her top away they are soon back to kissing before it's even hit the ground. Fingers fumble at shirt buttons and belt buckles.

All of a sudden, Jared stops her, saying he can't do this.

"What's wrong?" she asks concerned.

Jared stares at the floor. Unable to make eye contact.

"Jared, it's okay," she says gently stroking his face. "It's me."

A solitary tear trickles down his cheek. He forces himself to look her in the eye.

"Thank you," says Jared.

"I don't understand," Aubrey replies.

They rest their foreheads together. He takes a deep breath… then tells her to wake up.

Aubrey blinks. Groggy and disoriented. Adrift by a tidal wave of confusion. She looks at Jared as he hangs his head. Then looking down she realizes she's stood in her bra.

WHACK… she slaps him hard across the face. Grabs her top and storms out. Jared flinches as the front door slams and the foundations shudder from the force.

* * * * *

The next morning, Jared leans on some bridge railings overlooking a gorgeous view of a vast lake. The locket is open between his fingers. Inside is a photo of Aubrey alongside on of him.

He leaves the locket on the ledge and turns to walk away down a leafy path.

Unbeknownst to him, a girl walks up to the same spot to look out across the lake. She spots the necklace and sees him walking away.

"Excuse me?... EXCUSE ME?" she calls out.

Jared stops. He looks back.

"Is this yours?" asks the girl.

Jared ponders for a moment… then shakes his head.

"But it's got your picture inside it," she adds.

Jared is tongue-tied. He tries to think of a way to save face.

"You know," says the girl. "I reckon if you threw it from here, there wouldn't be much chance of seeing it on Ebay later!"

Jared saunters back, a little embarrassed. The girl tells him to be brave as she hands him the locket.

Jared looks out across the lake and then lobs the necklace as far as he can.

Splash... it disappears under the surface and

sinks below a tiny ripple. He is as still as a statue but has gone pale.

"How do you feel?" asks the Girl. "Please tell me you're not gonna dive in after it. I'm not a strong swimmer, so you'd have two drownings on your conscience."

"It's okay, I'm alright," he replies.

"Promise you won't run back as soon as I'm out of sight."

"I promise."

Jared starts to move away but pauses.

"Do I know you from somewhere?" he asks. "You look familiar!"

"That can't be your best chat up line?" she responds laughingly.

"Oh no, it's not a line. I…" he squirms.

"It's all right. I'm only messing with you!" she interjects.

Jared exudes a nervous laugh. Pivots and starts to saunter away from the bridge.

"You know," says the girl. "There's this cafe at

the bottom of the hill. Do you want to try some other lines out on me?"

"Oh, I erm... am probably not the best company at the moment."

"Oh, right, sure... with the whole locket thing."

"Sorry."

"That's alright. I won't jump off, I promise."

Jared laughs. "Well, err... have a good day. Thanks for the help with…"

"Sure. Anytime."

As Jared turns away, he finds himself smiling.

The girl watches as he starts to wander off. She ponders for a moment then takes a mobile phone out of her pocket and plays a ringtone...

It's the tune, *'You are my Sunshine'*.

He stops still. A wave of confusion washes over him.

Finding his bearings, he checks his pocket, panics, then rushes back to the railings, searching high and low. The girl has turned away, as if minding her own business.

"Excuse me, miss?" he asks. "You haven't seen a necklace, have you? One of those heart-shaped lockets."

"I can't see anything. Did you leave it here?" she asks.

"Err... you know I can't remember."

"Did it mean a lot to you?"

Jared contemplates, before saying, "Not anymore."

He turns to leave, but for some reason he can't understand, he finds himself asking the girl if he knows her from somewhere.

"That can't be your best chat up line?" she replies.

"Oh no, it's not a line, I…"

"It's alright, I'm just messing with you!"

He blushes. Motions to leave but twists back within seconds.

"There's this cafe at the bottom of the hill," he says. "Do you fancy a coffee?"

The girl smiles, playing it cool.

"Err, sure... okay. By the way, I'm Leondra.

© *Richard Dunford*

Image Copyright to Pen & Ink Designs Publishing

SISTERS

Putting her nose out of the door, Hazel pulled a face at the sight of the damp, drizzling, slowly falling rain before her, before tightening the scarf around her neck. Then, with a sigh, she stepped out onto her pathway, thinking, 'How many times have I taken this walk over the last ten years? Is this all there is to my life now?'

Her steps were slow, her mind reflective, as she took at the familiar sights that she saw every morning on her way to work.

The gate hanging lopsidedly off its hinge at No 10, with the beautiful lilac tree, abundantly in bud and overhanging the fence.

Mrs. Patrick and her daughter, Julie waiting at the bus stop for their usual early morning bus, while their black cat watched dolefully from the front room window anticipating another day alone until their return.

And Molly, the cleaner at The Bridge Public House, having a sneaky smoke on the back steps. All of these usually provided a sense of contentment when Hazel took the towpath, a short-cut route to her job as a therapist at the local Medical Centre.

Today however, her mood felt flat and strangely unsettled. She asked herself yet again, what on earth was wrong with her?

She wasn't dissatisfied with her life. No, not in the least, she reflected. In fact, she was quite proud of the way, following the loss of her parents, that she had turned her life around. Despite the strange disappearance and desertion of her sister, Paula. Having thrown herself into her work, it had brought her great satisfaction, helping others in the way she did.

However, an increasing sense of anticipation had started pervading her thoughts for at least a week. Almost as if her life was about to drastically change. Yet, she wasn't sure how – wasn't sure what she should be looking for.

She realised that since the trauma of her loss, and as part of her recovery, she had become de-sensitised, burying many of the hurtful emotions.

'So much for my skills as a therapist. I should learn to practice what I preach,' she thought, walking on. Could it be that the protective fog she had built around her had begun to clear?

Physically shrugging off the idea, she stepped up her pace.

A familiar jogger, barely breathing heavily at the effort, approached her, moving with strong gazelle-like strides. She had seen him many times, admiring his strength and resilience. As he passed, she noticed his focus on his task.

He never stopped to say, 'Good Day.'

Taking a leaf from his book she attempted to put a spring into her step!

Rounding a blind bend in the path, she stopped short. A bedraggled, soaking wet, deep brown dog was blocking her path, looking out over the canal. He was not moving, just staring.

With some anticipation she slowly approached, taking in the scene around her. She was wary of anyone who might be lurking in the bushes, so peered into the shrubbery to check if someone might be injured but could see nothing unusual. She noticed the dogs' fur was greying at the tips and was somewhat matted.

She didn't want to be late for work, but the

creature was in a pitiful state, being saturated and shivering. Approaching the dog, she gently talked to him. The creature seemed strangely familiar to her. However, he did not move or respond to her voice.

Hazel peered across the canal in the same direction as the dog. A barge, painted garishly in purple and pink, was tied up there. There was smoke curling gently out of a metal chimney stack. As she watched, a woman in denim dungarees and wellington boots came up on deck. She was carrying a watering can and proceeded to meticulously water several plant pots arranged artistically on the deck.

The dog at her side whimpered but still did not move. Hazel wondered if the dog belonged to this woman, so decided to ask.

"Hi," she shouted across the water. "Does this poor dog belong to you?" She waited a response, but none came. Irritated, she called again.

"Hellooow… this dog appears to be lost and is soaking wet. Is he yours?"

A long silence followed, but still no reply came from the woman who having been concentrating on her plants, had now taken up a broom to sweep off the deck.

Hazel decided to walk over the bridge to catch the attention of the woman. She patted the dog on the head, noticing a studded collar hidden in his fur. Taking hold of the collar, she felt a jolt of memory somewhere deep in her mind. Shivering from the experience, she started to move, giving the dog a gentle tug as she went. She need not have, as the dog turned and followed her without question.

Marvelling at the strangeness of this, Hazel walked to the bridge, murmuring reassuringly as she walked. The dog did not look at her, he just followed.

Coming down on the other side of the canal, the barge was now about 100 yards ahead of her. Hazel's pace slowed. Again, she experienced the weirdest sense of familiarity, causing her to stop in hesitation. The dog passed her and raced ahead.

At this point, she had almost decided to leave, feeling sure the dog had returned to its rightful owner, but instead, she walked on, somehow strongly drawn by the woman on the barge.

The dog stopped at the steps resting between the walkway and the side of the barge. As she came alongside, the woman had gone below deck. Hazel could hear the clattering of crockery and kitchen utensils coming from below. She visualised the woman cleaning up, taking pride in her waterway home.

Hazel spoke to the dog, saying, "On you get then, you are home now, go and get dry."

The dog looked at her briefly before doing as she bid.

He sat on the edge of the decking, watching Hazel as she turned to continue on her way to work. She could feel him still watching as she re-crossed the bridge. Stopping, she turned to look back. The dog was no longer on deck so she surmised he had gone below to get dried off.

When she last looked, the woman was again on deck, this time shouting, "Where are you? I won't leave 'til you come!"

'Weirder and weirder,' thought Hazel, now anxious that she was extremely late for her first appointment. Quickly she hurried on her way.

Work was just a typical day.

Old Harry Pendleton came in for his usual back massage which eased his arthritis. And for the two new Reflexology patients, who had been referred, she did a thorough assessment and devised treatment plans. Afterwards, she did her monthly stock check, made a list of replenishments, and caught up on her patient reports.

Due to her having been so busy, Hazel did not see any of her colleagues that day.

Strangely though, throughout her duties, Hazel had been constantly distracted by the morning's events prior to her arriving at work. The dog was on her mind, and she became determined, that on her way home that evening, she would check with the woman on the barge to ensure he was alright.

Locking her cabinet and treatment room door, Hazel made her way out of the Medical Centre to find the earlier drizzle still falling.

She wondered, 'Where is the promised sunshine?' It was early May and about time the weather was finer. Her thoughts turned to her decision to seek out the owner of the barge on her way home, so she set off determinedly to do so.

Approaching the bridge which crossed to the other side of the canal, Hazel could not immediately see the barge where it had been moored that morning. As she rose up the steps to cross, it was clear that the mooring was empty. The barge had gone.

Feeling suddenly tearful, empty, and cross with herself for not taking more action that morning, Hazel went back down the steps and continued on her way home. She hoped that the barge had just moved further along the canal, and that she might yet get a chance to check on the welfare of the dog.

Hazel spent a restless and lonely night. She had remained living in her parents' house after their death. After her sister had seemingly taken off somewhere due to her own grief, the house had become Hazel's retreat and solace.

The place was full of memories. There were many pictures of herself and her sister growing up. Playing in the garden, birthday parties on the lawn, jelly and ice-cream on Sundays. She decided to lift out the old family album to reminisce, something she had not had the inclination to do since the death of her parents.

With a hot cup of cocoa, she settled down to browse through the photos, full of mixed emotions, happy, sad, and bittersweet. Sitting in the armchair, she was only half a dozen pages in, when she fell asleep, dreaming of the dog and the woman on the boat.

Awaking with a start, Hazel realised she had slept heavily, never having made it to bed the night before. The photo album was on the floor and some photos had slipped out. She would have to re-fix them that evening.

Hurriedly washing and dressing, and after a quick cup of coffee, she was soon on her way with the door slamming shut behind her. The infernal drizzle was still coming down, making her feel irritated rather than reassured. When passing Mrs. Patrick and Julie at the bus stop, she didn't bother to say her usual, 'Good Morning!'

Molly was already putting out her sneaky cigarette at the back door of The Bridge as Hazel stepped onto the tow path, an indication that she was definitely late. And to confirm it, the jogger was nearly at the end of the tow path.

'Oh crikey,' she thought to herself, *'I must get a move on!'*

Rounding the blind bend in a hurry, Hazel's heart jumped in her breast with surprise. There was the dog again, not waiting for her obviously because he did not look in her direction as she approached. But, he was doing it again, staring across the canal, and there it was – the barge was moored up in the same spot!

Her bile rising, Hazel decided this time she must take action. It was ridiculous that the dog was out on the towpath, wet through and bedraggled again, what was the woman thinking?

Almost running to the bridge and crossing it, she realised the dog was immediately behind her, like a shadow. On the crest of the bridge, she paused to check the barge again, and sure enough, the woman was out brushing the deck.

Hazel called out sharply, "Hey, your dog is here and is all wet through again!"

The woman momentarily paused her sweeping, but again no reply was forthcoming. Incensed, Hazel almost sprinted across the bridge and down the other side. However, by the time she was within distance of the barge, the woman had gone below deck.

Even though she was hurrying to reach to the craft, the dog had somehow overtaken her and was sitting on the barge steps. She could hear the woman clattering around in the kitchen below, just like the day before. Hazel hesitated, not sure whether to board or not.

Losing her nerve, Hazel decided to peep through one of the small windows of the barge. One which was propped open by a photograph frame. As she looked at the photograph, her jaw dropped – it was of her parents! What was this woman doing with a photograph of her parents? Reeling with shock, she heard the clattering in the kitchen stop, then the woman called out, "Ok, I know you are there – are you coming in this time or not?"

Bewildered and feeling a little panic-stricken, Hazel ran back to the bridge. She was confused and agitated so keeping running, she crossed the bridge, only looking back when she reached the other side. Again, the dog had gone inside. Hazel decided there was something very strange about all of this, so she needed to think things through.

Approaching the door of the Medical Centre, she felt dizzy and disorientated. The door was locked, no-one was there? Had she inadvertently turned up for work on a Bank Holiday? What was happening to her? She would go home and sleep.

Arriving home, Hazel leaned against the door

for minutes before opening it. On her hurried walk back from work, she noticed the barge had again moved from its mooring, and there was no sign of the dog.

More confused than ever, she made for the kitchen to make a hot drink, which she took to bed, sleeping solidly for hours. When she woke, she thought through the last couple of days and intuitively knew the events were significant for her. As she went downstairs, she thought to herself, *'The fog is definitely clearing.'*

Entering the lounge, where she intended to replace the photos in the album she had dropped on the floor last night, she received yet another shock. The album was not there. She knew she had not picked it up that morning – she had not had time to do so. She checked the table, then the cupboard, but the album was missing.

Becoming quite frantic, Hazel rushed upstairs to dress and within minutes found herself on the way to the towpath. She did not understand why, she just knew she needed to go there. The vision of the photograph on the barge and the strangely familiar woman haunted her. Dreading she would not find the barge moored in its usual spot she ran all the way.

Breathlessly approaching the bridge Hazel thankfully saw that not only was the barge moored up, but the dog was sitting on the decking. He was watching her approach. She slowed her pace over the crest of the bridge, and there tied to the railings she saw were some beautiful wildflowers.

Inexplicably, Hazel could feel the tears freely running down her face. Suddenly she experienced the greatest sense of relief as she was drawn towards the barge.

Approaching the barge, Hazel could see lit lanterns and candles inside. It looked so warm and welcoming. Still, the dog seemed very wet, but he did not move from the decking of the barge, he just watched and waited. From the open window of the barge, she could hear music playing. The tune pulled hauntingly at her heart strings It was something familiar from her childhood. Debating what to do next she decided, before knocking to speak to the woman, to look through the window again, as she had done that morning.

Hanging over the photo-frame of her parents on the windowsill, was an old dog's collar, with studs in it. Next to it was a newspaper cutting.

The headline read…

"Bereaved Therapist Jumps from Canal Bridge, and
Dog Tries to Save Her!"

© *L M Handley*

Images licensed to Pen & Ink Designs Publishing

THE JOB

I rushed towards the elevator, immediately regretting wearing my red ruby high heels as my foot slipped out of the back. I had ten minutes to get to the 17th floor for my interview. My whole life had been planned around this moment as I wanted nothing more than to work for the most prestigious fashion magazine in the world. This had always been my dream; to sit behind a large desk facing a beautiful view of the city around me.

'I bet you can see the best view in the whole city from those windows,' I thought.

Growing up I had attended three fashion and design schools - graduating with honors from each one. If I didn't get this job, I would just die! I knew it was silly planning my entire life around a single job. I had heard from everyone I had ever revealed my dreams to, how naive and irresponsible it was.

I waited impatiently as I pressed the glowing yellow buttons next to the elevator, tapping my foot with a loud clank every time my heels met the polished tiled floor. I watched as the elevator counted down, stopping on every floor. It felt as if a decade had passed by the time it finally reached the ground floor and the doors opened with a welcoming ding.

Stepping inside, I moved over as a woman with skin the color of cocoa beans walked into the elevator, pressing the 15th floor button. She wore bright beautiful colours that complimented her skin. She looked at me and smiling widely nodded her head in my direction, as if to say hello.

Pushing the 17th-floor button I let out the breath I was holding. I was going to make it to the interview after all. I knew there would probably be dozens of people applying for the same job, and maybe some of them were more qualified than me. But I was determined and just wouldn't take no for an answer as I was born for this job, and that was the one thing I was certain of most in this world.

I let out a small squeal when the elevator stopped. We were just above the 13th floor; the light was half lit on the number twelve so I pressed the 17th floor button again. I pressed it three times to be exact. The last time my finger turning a dark red where I had used all my might to push the button in.

"It will do no good," announced the woman standing in the elevator. She turned to me, looking so sure of herself, and looking at me she said, "The elevator is stuck."

"How do you know? Are you an elevator expert? If so please get me to the 17th floor," I said, sounding more demanding than I was trying to be.

"I have been stuck in elevators quite a few times. When I lived in Africa the constant blackouts due to the wars would knock the elevators out of service, sometimes for hours, and one time we were stuck in an elevator for an entire day!" the woman explained. "I can assure you; I would rather be stuck in this elevator than one there any day."

She sounded so calm, even though I had begun pacing the floor, growing increasingly frantic. This was a once-in-a-lifetime opportunity, and they wouldn't accept excuses no matter the reason.

'If I don't get out of this elevator soon, I can kiss my life goodbye!' I thought. Looking at her I saw her warm brown eyes watching me curiously.

"It will be okay," she assured me, "someone will come to help us soon."

"I can't wait for soon!" I declared. "I need to get to the 17th floor, **now**! You don't understand if I am late for that interview I will never get the job. The job I have worked my whole life to get."

The woman looked at me before responding, "What I came here to do is important as well, but there is nothing we can do but wait."

I pressed my back against the back of the elevator and slowly slid my body down the wood until I was sitting on the floor. Slipping the red heels off I threw one at the door, knowing I was acting like a child, but I couldn't help it. I just couldn't believe this was happening.

Sitting feeling sorry for myself for quite some time, I suddenly realised that it wasn't getting me anywhere so I looked at the stranger who was now sitting across from me. Her eyes were closed, her head resting against the wall.

"What is your name?" I asked breaking the silence.

"Lena," she replied, sounding surprised I had spoken to her.

"My name is Amanda. It's nice to meet you," I said, trying to be polite and make up for my breakdown earlier.

"You said you lived in Africa for some time? What was that like?" I asked, admitting that I had never travelled but had always wanted to.

"It's a beautiful land with exotic animals. Most of the people are lovely as well but there are some there who are so corrupt by their own vision of what their life should be that it has clouded their judgment, robbing them of their compassion."

"Where are you from?" she asked me in return.

"I have lived my whole life here, in the city," I admitted, feeling closer to the elevator than ever.

"Can I ask what you are doing here?" I didn't mean to be rude, but I always was curious. I think I inherited that trait from my mother, but my dad always said we were just plain nosey so tried to make it sound less prying by saying we were just curious.

"I was headed to the 15th floor. My lawyer and I are meeting with the fashion magazine editors today."

"Your lawyer? Are you suing them or something?" I asked in a joking manner.

"Actually, yes I am," she responded as she tilted her head up, wearing a proud expression.

"What could you possibly want to sue the best fashion company in the world for?" I asked, feeling enraged as if she was sitting there telling me that she was suing me personally.

She grew frigid and straightened out her shoulders. "Not that it's any of your business but, I am suing them for objectifying women."

"I would hardly call displaying the most fashionable high heels and make-up trends objectifying!" I declared.

"Well, I am not suing them for showing shoes or makeup products. I am suing them for making every little girl and teenager who, at such an impressionable age, seems to think that they have to look and act in a certain way. Or be a certain height or weight to be beautiful. Did you know, that in the United States, 20 million women suffer from a clinically significant eating disorder at some time in their life? Where do you think it all starts? With magazines like these. Ones that promote nothing but slander against the women of today, so, they should be banned!"

I rubbed the back of my head, admitting that I had had no idea that so many women suffered from such diseases.

An awkward silence filled the elevator and I struggled to find what to say to the passionate stranger.

"Let me ask you something," she asked, breaking the silence.

I nodded as she began asking her question, letting her know I was listening.

"If this elevator gets fixed in time for your interview, and let's just say you do get the job, can you honestly live with yourself knowing, that you, are part of an organization that not only sells sex to young woman but throws images of what and who they should, be in their faces. All while knowing they can never match up to those photoshopped expectations?"

She left a pause, allowing the question to sink in before continuing, "I volunteered at an eating disorder clinic for seven years! I have seen all kinds of suffering, and no, the magazines aren't the sole blame, but they are the start. I don't know how many young people I spoke with who just wanted to be perfect. Just like those women featured in this magazine. If you take this job, you are not only doing an injustice to yourself, but you are also doing an injustice to the young impressionable women all around you."

Thinking about it, I admit that I had never been more relieved than I was when the elevator started moving once again and I was finally separated from this judgmental stranger.

Arriving at my floor I made my way from the elevator to the front desk where a woman sat with large rim glasses and bright red lipstick.

"Excuse me. I had an interview scheduled for today, but I got stuck in the elevator," I told her.

She looked up at me through the top of her glasses, clearly annoyed that I was there, before pointing her index finger towards the back of the room, and instructing me, "Go down that hallway."

I quickly made my way down the hallway and walked into an empty room where a tall blonde was sitting behind her desk speaking on her phone.

"Let me call you back, Betty," she said and hung up the phone, instructing me to take a seat in a single leather sofa chair in front of her desk.

"I understand that you were stuck in the elevator. That had to be miserable," she said, sounding not the least bit interested in how miserable I was.

I looked around me as she walked me through the interview process. I could see large prints of the past months' magazine covers plastered across the wall.

I don't know where my next question came from, but I spoke over her, asking, "Would you ever consider featuring a large-figured woman in one of your magazines?"

For a few moments she sat looking at me, a confused look on her face. "What, like a fat person," she asked, and a look of dismay crossed her face.

I finally realised what the stranger in the elevator had been telling me. These people were all the same, selling impossible perfection and beauty to women who were already beautiful.

Standing up from the chair I did the one thing I thought I would never do. Looking at the interviewer, who was staring at me wide-eyed and curious, I announced, "If you will excuse me, I don't think this job is for me," and I quickly walked out of the room and back to the elevators, hoping this time I wouldn't get stuck.

Thankfully, I was out of the elevator and on the ground floor in minutes.

Walking through the lobby I stopped when I spotted the same woman from the elevator.

She waved at me, calling out, "Did you get the job?"

"No," I said. "I decided I wasn't going to work for a company that objectifies women."

A bright smile spread across her face from ear to ear and coming close she wrapped her arm through mine before pulling a card from her pocket and handing it to me.

Looking at it, my heart began to race as I read, 'Love your Body Magazine.' She was the chief editor and creator of the magazine.

"I know it's not the job you came here for," she said, "but, it's yours if you'll have it."

I pulled her into an unexpected hug, thanked her, then hurried outside to call my mother. Finally, I had done what I had come to do and that was to get a job at a high-ranking fashion magazine. I was just so grateful to the stranger in the elevator for opening my eyes into seeing that no amount of money was worth objectifying women.

'Now to explain all this to my mother,' I thought as I pulled my phone from my pocket and dialed her number. I felt happier and more accomplished at how I had stood up for myself. For once in my life, I had listened to someone who had different beliefs to me. She had opened my eyes to the world around me. As I walked out of that building not only did I have a job, but I also had a new-found respect for myself and the women all around me.

© *Julie Wall*

Images licensed to Pen & Ink Designs Publishing

WRITER IN RESIDENCE

I'm a writer: and certain words fascinate me. For example - voluptuous and intransigence. For me, creation is a heady experience with endless possibilities.

'She was voluptuous in her intransigence.'

There. I can be pretty confident no one has written that sentence before. Mind you, I am not sure what to do with it though.

Characters also intrigue me. Imagine a young woman with glossy dark hair standing before a tall mirror. I will call her, Mrs. Brusque-Mantel.

She has an older friend, a Mrs. Derailleur, who visits twice a week for afternoon tea. Her husband does something 'in the city,' but I don't yet know what.

It's pleasant work, sitting here in the study overlooking the long garden with its laden plum trees and the distant view of the mountains. But it can also be frustrating. Making decisions, I mean.

Decision such as, what colour is Mrs. Brusque-Mantel's adorable little dress? What breed is her dog, and what name shall I give it?

I smoke a Camel, stare at the mountains, and ponder these queries I must decide upon.

Then there are the finicky issues of punctuation and emphasis. For example.

What if I were to write…

'Certain words fascinate me as I'm a writer.'

Or, alternatively I could write…

'As a writer, I am fascinated by certain words.'

Now, what do you think? Which comment is preferable. The original or the alternative?

To me it is obviously the alternative.

My apologies, I know I shouldn't be talking to you. Addressing you like this is in fact crass and old-fashioned. Before I know it, I'll be asking something daft such as - Reader, should she marry him?

It's just that writing is a lonely business. You see, I'm unlikely to get much of a response from my daily companions. That's the table, the keyboard, those two ceramic coasters, and that absurd photograph next to the pot of sharpened pencils.

Interruptions are the worst of it. You get a sudden inspiration that unlocks your imagination's door, then it's…

"Elizabeth, have you been in my study?"

"No my dear – why?" It's Henry my husband.

"Where's Adam?"

"At Simon's doing prep."

"And Florence?"

"It's Saturday – her riding lesson. Why, Henry? What's the matter?"

"Someone's been on the computer. My table's disturbed, and there's a sheet of gibberish in the printer."

Henry Kemp stumps back upstairs, hating them all. He has worked hard to provide them with this home. The children have spacious bedrooms, his wife has her sewing closet. Each has a laptop. And yet they repay him with this ingratitude – the violation of his sanctuary.

Back in his study, Henry tidies his desk, ensuring there is an equal space between each object. The pot of pencils, coasters for his drinks, and a photograph of his father in uniform. There is a speck of what looks like dandruff on the desk's polished surface. He does not have dandruff; it is forbidden. He quickly whisks it away with a cloth.

He glances again at the sheet he has found in the printer tray.

Brusque-Mantel / Mrs. Derailleur / voluptuous in her intransigence.

'What nonsense is this?' he thinks. Possibilities rush through his mind as he strokes his moustache nervously.

Maybe someone is playing a joke. Perhaps their mansion has become a centre of espionage, and this was a message left by an agent. If so, who was the intended recipient? Perhaps his wife is somehow involved. She is a woman so singularly dull how could she be hiding a secret?

The Financial Times is a temporary distraction, so he scans it for news of the Kilmartin deal. If there is movement, he needs to get on to Frobisher at once. But his mind is distracted by a word from the mysterious text. It lingers long after he has torn the paper into pieces.

Voluptuous!

* * * * *

That afternoon Mrs. Raleigh will be calling on Elizabeth. The thought makes Henry's heart race.

He jumps up and strides to the window, cracking his knuckles in nervous excitement. He imagines her approaching the house through the garden. Her hips are swaying, her blonde hair partly hidden by a cream-coloured, broad-brimmed hat.

Why does his wife never wear high-heeled shoes like those? The last time Mrs. Raleigh had visited he was sure she had given him 'a certain look.'

And the way she ate her chocolate gateau!

Raleigh must be a feeble sort of cove. No, a sad business brain, having lost a lot of money in the Central Bank crash, the idiot. Weak handshake. Not the kind of man for a woman who devours her cake in that way. Whereas he…

The phone rang. It was Frobisher about the Kilmartin deal, but he could scarcely concentrate.

He was so distracted by a vision of Lydia Raleigh peeling a banana.

"So, it's agreed," Frobisher was saying. "I'll send someone round with the papers later today."

"Papers?" But Frobisher had rung off.

In his basement gym, Henry prepared in earnest for his wife's friend's visit. Thirty minutes on the exercise bike was followed by forty minutes on the rowing machine, then twenty press-ups, and a punch bag session that, in his mind, involved Mrs. Raleigh's husband.

He imagined greeting Lydia in a singlet soaked in a real man's sweat. Then he thought better of it and went for a shower.

* * * * *

Characters can be a nuisance. It's unfortunate that we need such troublesome creations, but we can't do without them. And they're expected to be

good because, being sociologically nuanced, they can't be thoroughly nasty, or utterly good, because such extremes don't ring true.

Don't they?

Well, in 'real life' (whatever that is) I've known people who possess not one redeeming feature. Not one. Men often appear to be terminally arrogant and innately conceited and unfaithful. Those who trample over the weak and who humiliate their wives. Greedy, intolerant, self-centered, and vain, they bully colleagues and browbeat their families.

And yet, I've known women, kindly, loving women, who live with such brutes. Their hours are spent among children, who they strive to protect from these men. When not with their babies they cook, clean, shop, and sew. And so it is that their days pass, falling like dry leaves from the beech tree in that garden through the window.

Say one day, on his way to work, the man is affable with his fellow travellers. Say he drops a ten-pound note into the greasy cap of the station busker. Imagine then, how he might come home that night with flowers for the woman he humiliated that morning. Do these things make him 'nuanced'? No, I think not for he is happy because yesterday he pulled off a deal that ruined thousands.

Take the Brusque-Mantels, my present subject. Her beauty was washed away by childbirth and her husband's cruelty. Yet, she remains a lovely woman.

Her glossy dark hair that crackles as the brush moves through it. A mouth, made by God for kissing. An unrequited mouth, one might think. But there is something in the eyes that hints at secrets.

While her husband, Bernard, preens himself for the arrival of Valerie Derailleur. He is liberal with the aftershave. He then flings wide his study window and inhales the air from his garden. He plans his strategy well, as if her visit is a board meeting.

He will 'send signals' in a manly way, making the agenda clear. She will respond with alacrity and gratitude. He will slip her his business card with his private number on. Deal done.

And all the while he will think his wife has seen none of this. A dull and stupid woman who will miss the glances, the look held longer than is needed, the card plucked from the waistcoat and secreted in the woman's glove. For such men, the world is a simple place. Their very motives drive nature itself, their power shapes all destinies.

Of course, as the creator of these people, I should keep my feelings out of it. Yet the truth is, I am half in love with Helen Brusque-Mantel. She reminds me of an American I once knew, whose

Mexican husband took her to live in Chiapas. There, on the steaming edge of Guatemala, her beauty drained away in tears.

As a writer, I can't cope with Mexico, so I have brought her to England. Here is where her beauty will drain away in tears. Therefore, if my treatment of Helen appears subjective, I ask your forgiveness.

Similarly with her husband, the pernicious buffoon. I promise that if the opportunity arises to present these people as 'rounded' I shall seize it.

Finally, the plot. I have set up a situation where Valerie Derailleur and the Brusque-Mantels are in the house together, but, what is the outcome?

Mmm…. I wonder?

Is the blonde visitor everything she seems? Is she, in fact, an industrial spy, employed by a rival company? Is she an assassin, hired by a ruined ex-colleague to wreak revenge? Could there, in her Reiss handbag among the make-up tubes and lipsticks nestles a stiletto?

I am sorry you must wait, and you'll find out.

* * * * *

"What time are you expecting the Raleigh woman?" Henry asks.

Resisting the temptation to respond with, *'None of your damn business, you swine,'* Elizabeth says, "Three o'clock," as she continues ironing.

He takes a sideways glance at the stack of clothes on the kitchen table. "Don't know why we can't get a maid to do that – I've offered, for God's sake."

"It's no trouble. Besides, women enjoy ironing, you know."

To date, Henry had seduced two maids and the au pair. A fourth sordid affair was out of the question.

He stood in the doorway, hands in his pockets, watching her with a sort of pity. Despite the money she had brought to the marriage, she still had something of the peasant about her. She bent over the board, almost humbly, moving the iron across the sleeve of a shirt in a dumb mechanical movement. Her broad flat slippers made her look like a duck.

He thought of Lydia Raleigh. Of course, such a woman wouldn't iron, but if she did, she would do it glamorously, in Simone platform shoes by Lipsy.

"Thought I might pop in and say hello," he said casually. "Just briefly you understand."

"Whatever you say, dear."

"Frobisher's sending some papers round at two-thirty, but that won't take long. They just need signing."

"Working on a Saturday," she said. "Such dedication."

He looked at her sharply, thinking he detected a surprising note of sarcasm. But her meek repetitive movements made him dismiss the idea. Irony required an imaginative intelligence, something his wife did not possess.

Mechanically she continued her work, never looking up, locked into a bent submission by his presence. If only he would go away. She wanted to breathe, to lift her eyes to the blessed space he would leave behind him. The iron hissed contempt in small explosions of steam.

As it happened, Frobisher's man was late arriving with the papers. It being almost three when he sat down at his study table to check them. At that moment the doorbell rang.

At last, Lydia Raleigh!

Hurriedly he signed the documents, before practically bundling the courier down the stairs in time to see, from the rear, those hips swaying into the lounge.

"Ah, Mrs. Raleigh," he said, leeringly.

"Oh, Mr. Kemp," she said, simperingly in return.

Her white poodle careered about the room in frantic joy.

"Poppy, you naughty thing."

Henry imagined her speaking to him like that and the thought made him breathless. They sat and talked.

He feigned a careless, masculine pose, while his wife seemed nervous, perching stiffly on the edge of her seat. Lydia inhabited the chair with her curves. She was fragrant, relaxed, while occasionally addressing the now-sleeping Poppy in a low, pouting voice.

He found himself ridiculously saying, "Would she like a biscuit?" Almost adding, 'And for yourself - a banana?'

As if on cue, his wife went to make tea. Lydia shifted on her chair, revealing more leg.

"I so like Elizabeth's adorable little dress. It's so…" she hesitated tantalisingly - "adorable."

He was now convinced she desired him. Why else would she mention his wife's dress?

"How is your husband?" he asked. "Business doing well, I hope."

'Why talk of him? It's you I want, you beast!'

At least, that is what Henry was imagining he had heard.

What she actually said, was, "Poppy, come to Mama." The poodle awoke and scampered to her, sitting at the glowing edge of her stilettoes, her muzzle stiffly raised, while she fed it morsels of biscuit. The dog tongued her vermillion-tipped fingers with greedy pleasure.

He watched, unable to speak.

Then, hearing the clink of cups from the kitchen, he said in a rush, "I wonder if you'd like my card. My personal details, etcetera."

"Why not?" she said, sending him a look that set

his heart racing.

When Elizabeth returned with the tea a desultory conversation ensued. There was a tension in the room that Henry put down to animal magnetism – not Poppy's, but his.

It must, he thought, be a strain for the two women to inhabit the same space. Old prey and new prey sipping Darjeeling together in the presence of the hunter.

Lydia Raleigh lifted the delicate China cup from its saucer and Henry followed every inch of its progress to her mouth. She drank with sensual enjoyment, closing her eyes, sighing, as she said, "Ah, so delicious." The cup, when she put it down, carried a new design: at its lip a bright vermillion stain.

Breaking the silence, he asked, "So, where do you get your pins? – er, I mean - your shoes."

"Oh," she said casually, "sometimes Kurt Geiger, occasionally Nicholas Kirkwood." Then, breathily, "I get my Gina's from Harrods."

Henry, momentarily overcome, closed his eyes. I get my Gina's from Harrods. It was the most exciting thing he had heard any woman say, being delivered in a tone that promised untold delights.

So preoccupied was he with Lydia's teacup, her voice, and her heels, that he ignored his wife completely. Thus, he failed to see the jealous anger his interest had provoked.

He got up and went out, ostensibly to visit the bathroom but, in reality, it was to get the business card from his study.

* * * * *

Endings. The writer's curse. Even more challenging than the deadline and the word count. Whether characters participate in great deeds or are simply lounging about, they have to be finished off. An outcome is what everyone demands, but in real life (whatever that is) things rarely end neatly.

Bernard Brusque-Mantel, that contemptible worm, needs his comeuppance. But, perhaps, on the very brink, a surprising act of goodness saves him.

And is Helen, that paragon of virtue, discovered at the end to be a monster? As for the alluring Valerie, what is her role exactly in all this?

I'm working on it with the help of my last

Camel.

* * * * *

Henry knew someone had been in his study again. The computer was on and the window was half shut. The odour of Turkish tobacco lingered in the air. But being too preoccupied with thoughts of Lydia he hardly noticed.

He found a business card and ran lightly downstairs. The door to the lounge was ajar. There was something beyond that was not quite silence – a breathy intensity, a suppressed groan. He opened the door wide.

Lydia Raleigh was bending over his wife's chair, her mouth on his wife's mouth. Elizabeth's long white throat was arched, and she was responding, greedily. It was not until he spoke that they even noticed his presence.

"My… God, you're…" stammered Henry.

"Yes, lovers!" the Raleigh woman exclaimed, sneering, and exultant.

He felt an overwhelming urge to kick the dog. And had Poppy been closer his boot would have propelled her through the French window like a world-class Number Ten.

Instead, he spoke in an oddly strained voice, "How dare you? In my house of all places. I'll divorce you for this!"

"Good," said Elizabeth, who was now holding Lydia's hand. "The children and I are leaving you anyway." And, as an afterthought, she added, "You utter brute."

"Don't think you'll get any of my money," he said, shouting now.

"What money?" said the Raleigh woman, in a tone that was both brazen and unsettling.

Enraged, shaking, he strode from the room and up to his study. He needed to calm himself and take stock. In the computer printer tray was a sheet of paper. It appeared to be a story of some kind. He glanced at the final paragraph.

Unable to face his triple failure – as husband, lover, and businessman - Bernard Brusque-Mantel went into the garden and hanged himself from a bough of the beech tree.

Henry screwed up the paper and threw it into the waste bin. Bloody cheek! As if adultery wasn't enough, the pair of them resorted to these childish practical jokes.

The phone rang. It was Frobisher with an apology.

"Sorry about not sending the papers around. Spot of uncertainty in the markets. Just as well we held off – the whole outfit's gone down the pan. If we'd signed, we'd have been wiped out."

The breeze from the window suddenly felt cold. "Are you saying you didn't send a courier?"

Outside dusk fell. He sat in the gloom, unable to move. Ruined. Soon he heard laughter coming from the garden and went to the window to look. Elizabeth and Lydia Raleigh stood at the gate kissing. A car pulled up and someone got out. They shook hands. There was more laughter.

Each turned and looked up at his window. He now recognized the driver. It was the man who had brought the papers, claiming to be from Frobisher.

He spent the night on a chair in his study. A full moon filled the room with pallid disdain. Towards dawn, he tipped the waste bin's contents onto the table. He found the screwed-up sheet, straightened it out, and read again the last few lines.

So, that's me more or less done. Mission accomplished as they say.

* * * * *

You know, in the end, I felt quite sorry for Brusque-Mantel, despite the absence of a single redeeming feature. The image of him rummaging in the tool shed for a length of sturdy rope will remain with me for some time.

But now I must take myself and my briefcase off to pastures new. I am in need of a fresh commission, a fresh residence. I wonder, would you be interested?

I promise not to use real names or make a mess.

I can be very discreet. You'll hardly know I'm there. Well, what do you say?

© *Julian Holt*

Images licensed to Pen & Ink Designs Publishing

STRAWBERRY FOOL

Stephen lets me do some gardening. It's all first names here. I have my own beds. They have also helped me out with the big bags of compost. But, as long as I show my receipts they let me buy whatever plants I want. My favourites are peonies. They remind me of her.

I arrive at half past eight in the morning every Monday, Wednesday, and Friday, taking a break for my elevenses.' Later, I pack up at a quarter to one, meaning I am home for the one o'clock news.

When Stephen arrives, he always salutes me. He must think I've been a military man. I've never bothered to correct him. However, I was never called up, on account of the accident.

It's pretty miserable weather today. I'm sure they'd let me inside to have my tea and digestives if I asked. To be honest the woman on reception has offered in the past, but, as I said to her, a little rain never did anyone any harm.

She'd laughed and said, "As long as you aren't the wicked Witch of the West?" She's a card that one.

Still, I'm happy perching on the upturned wheelbarrow. She shouts out the window, "We'll have to get you a fishing rod and a gnome's hat." I smile. Told you she was funny.

The joints are playing up today. Mustn't grumble. At eighty-seven I'm only too pleased to be alive. Many of the residents here are younger than me. It's the wet weather that does it. Sets off my rheumatism. I know many people think autumn is a depressing time of year. Yet I just see it as Mother Nature recharging her batteries.

I used to go 'conkering' as a lad. I had one that just kept on winning. I must have won twenty matches with it. Then it started to crack.

That was the year her family moved into the village. There were three daughters, but I'd only got eyes for Ellen. Her family had caused quite a stir. The father liked his drink, so he was arrested a couple of times. He also never seemed able to hold a job down long enough. Their mother took in mending and washing which somehow kept food on the table for them.

We only had two classes at our school. A married couple ran it in those days. She was in charge of the little ones where they just played, and he taught the other class, trying to prepare us for secondary school. He also gave extra lessons and homework to the ones he reckoned had a chance of getting into the local grammar school.

They didn't bother with me. I was bigger than all the others, even the older ones. He'd get me moving furniture, and when he spotted I had a talent for growing things he would let me weed the school gardens.

That was until my mother found out. One day she marched me down to the school and tore a right strip off him.

I can still remember her voice now, as she said to him, "I send my Thomas to school so that you can knock some sense into him. God knows I've tried. He's a kind soul but God never doled out his share of brains. If I wanted him to pull up dandelions, I've plenty of them on the farm at home." She feared nobody.

From that day on the teacher tried extra hard with me but, for some reason, the letters made no sense to me. They were all a jumble to my eyes.

Ellen thought was smart. When she joined our class, the teacher never had enough books for her. Her sisters were clever too, but she was the brightest. Even I could tell that. She finished everything the teacher set her. She'd wait by his desk while he marked her sums, never getting one wrong.

My numbers book was like a one-sided game of noughts and crosses.

He used to give her jobs to do in the classroom. Ellen picked some peonies out of somebody's front garden and gave them to the teacher on his birthday. He blushed. She would count the dinner money and if he ever needed a messenger she was asked to take it.

I was struggling with my work, so one morning he told Ellen to sit with me.

"Can't you do this? A big lad like you!"

I blushed.

"I could do this when I was four. How old are you? Twelve, thirteen? Have they kept you back because you're simple?"

"I'm nine. Just big for my age."

"What does your mother feed you? Whatever it is, it does the trick."

I loved the way she laughed, even if it was at my expense. I couldn't follow when she explained how to do the sums. In the end, she just told me the answers. It was strange to see ticks in my book the next day.

However, I didn't dare approach her at playtimes. Ellen was never alone. It made me happy just to see her. I didn't need to speak with her. Besides, what would I say?

I was, therefore, surprised one morning, just before lining up to go into class, when one of her sisters passed me a note. I could just about make out the few words. I couldn't believe my good fortune. Ellen wanted to meet me in the woods after school.

She seemed to ignore me all day long. Whenever I looked across at her, she turned away. Maybe she was shy after all. I didn't mind because I would have her all to myself that afternoon. I would tell my mother I'd been kept back after school to repeat my work. That had happened plenty of times before.

I thought she'd wait for me when the school bell was rung but she rushed off. I was excited about finally being alone with her. I knew the part of the woods she meant. There was a rope swing over a little stream.

When I reached the spot, I was disappointed to see that she was not alone. Her sisters were whispering to her and there were quite a few other children from our class. Lots of them were grinning. I don't know exactly who else was there.

My mother pressed me for details later, but I only focused on Ellen.

She came towards me with a red scarf. "We're going to play a little game, Thomas." I don't really remember much after that.

She was egged on by the others. They were shouting and cheering. The wool felt scratchy over my eyes. She took me by the hand and then left me standing. She called me to follow her. But her voice seemed to be coming from all sorts of different directions. She must have climbed a tree as I could hear her calling from above my head. She wanted me to follow her, so I began to scale the tree.

I recalled the shape of it well and the location of the lowest branches. Then the others started shouting "Higher, higher!"

I must have been near the top.

The last thing I heard from her was "Over here," before the branch snapped and I fell.

The doctor told my mother I was lucky to be alive. My mother had a load of questions for me. She wanted to know who had done this to me. Who had been there in the woods, and whose idea was the blindfold. She had her suspicions, but I never betrayed Ellen. I just told her I was playing with the other children.

I was off school for months. My mother nursed me but couldn't seem to help mentioning all the extra work my accident had caused her.

Then one day she came into my room and announced, "You've got a visitor."

I knew she wasn't impressed.

Turning I saw Ellen standing near the window. The light was streaming through, and it seemed to make an orange halo around her abundant red hair.

I thought an angel had visited my bedroom. She

had a brown paper bag with a few pink stains from the contents inside.

"I picked these for you. I'll fetch more if you like them."

I recognised the strawberry smell. I didn't like them. I pretended I did because she'd done something kind for me. My mother hovered about on the landing. Ellen sat down on the chair next to my bed. She looked around the room. "You're lucky to have your own room."

My mother couldn't resist adding, "But not so lucky to have both his legs broken. The surgeon said they might never be straight again."

There was a long silence. I thought that Ellen might take this as her cue to leave but she carried on, "Everybody misses you at school. When will you be coming back?"

"The doctor says I might be back in the autumn."

My mother couldn't resist butting in again, "And missing out on the harvest work! August is our busiest month. I don't know how I'm going to cope!"

"My father could help if you need a farmhand," Ellen offered.

My mother just grunted and went downstairs.

Ellen leaned forwards and told me she had some news to tell me.

"My parents have just had a letter. I've won a scholarship to St Agnes. It's a school a long way away. I'll be a boarder."

I'd never heard of St Agnes before but whoever she was, I hated her. I couldn't even pretend to be happy for Ellen. I told her a lie and said I wasn't feeling well. The doctor had only said the previous day that I was making good progress but now I had a sickness in my stomach. Turning over in my bed towards the wall I had my back towards her. I was worried I might start crying and she'd tell everyone I was a baby.

She stood up to go. "I thought you'd be happy for me."

"I am," I mumbled, without turning towards her.

She must have been standing there for a couple of minutes. I'd hoped she'd left. But as I turned over in the bed and she was still there, standing in the doorway. She looked down at the floor and muttered "I'm sorry about your legs."

That was it. She never came to see me again.

I went back to school in September. I had crutches for a while but soon worked out how to get by without them. Ellen only came back in the holidays and then a few years later her family moved away from the village. Her Dad had left for good so Ellen's mother took her daughters to live nearer her mother. Hearing all this from my mother I feigned a lack of interest but inside I was desperate to hear anything about her.

By the time the war started, I was ready to leave school. There was no way that my services would ever be called upon. Although I did learn to walk independently I always had a pronounced limp but I got used to it. I spent the war years driving a bus.

I heard about Ellen from time to time. She got married and had a family. At least that's what my mother told me.

"She was the only girl you were ever soft on.

You can't trust people with ginger hair. She would've led you a merry dance."

I wanted to leap to Ellen's defence and explain her hair was strawberry blonde and that she was kind, deep down. But I didn't bother. There was no point in disagreeing with my mother. Once she had an idea fixed in her head there was no budging it. She had always had it in for Ellen and her family as soon as they moved into the village. Was always criticising their clothes, the way they spoke, or the fact that her mother didn't keep the front step clean.

My mother was right about one thing, though, there was never anyone else I was sweet on. It's daft really. I'm not saying I've lived a life of a monk over the years – no - I've had several lady friends during that time. It's just that there was nobody who made me feel the way she did. I didn't want to settle for second best.

* * * * *

I've finished for the morning. I just need to wash down my tools and sweep up. A car has arrived that I don't recognise. I know all the vehicles of the staff and regular visitors. This one is pretty full. Maybe it's a new resident. There was a death last week and they've had the decorators in, smartening up the room. Yes, I was right, there's an elderly woman in the passenger seat. Must be her daughter bringing all the belongings through. You'd think she'd attend to her mother first.

Finally, she opens the passenger door and releases her mother from her seat belt. The elderly woman simply sits and stares out in front of her. Several members of staff come out to assist and I overhear the daughter telling them about her mother over the old woman's head. The words 'dementia' and 'stroke' sit in the air.

Carefully, they lift the woman into a wheelchair. You'd think that one of them would have given her a blanket to cover her legs. It's turned chilly. As they pass me, the woman turns to face me. It can't be her. The hair is white. But the smile is the same.

* * * * *

The receptionist was surprised to see me back at the nursing home that afternoon.

"Doing some overtime, Thomas?"

I hardly noticed what she said to me. I just wanted to see Ellen again.

I smiled. "I would like to visit somebody. There was a lady who came in at lunchtime. I think I know her."

The receptionist joked about me being a dark horse and whether I needed a chaperone.

Ellen's room was on the first floor so I took the lift. As I waited for the doors to close I took a proper look in the mirror, checking my tie was straight. My mother had a put-down for all occasions. Today's would have been, 'There's no fool like an old fool.'

Ellen was lying in her bed. The journey must have exhausted her. I could see her fine hair spread out on her pillow as her eyes were facing the ceiling. I knocked on the door. There was an orderly putting her clothes away. She must have been from an agency as she didn't recognise me.

She simply said that she would leave us alone. Perhaps she thought I was her husband. I did have a bunch of flowers in my hand. She took the flowers from me, saying she would put the peonies in water.

I hovered in the doorway. Then I eventually plucked up the courage to go in.

Ellen did not turn her face towards me. I sat myself down in the chair by the window. The orderly came back with the flowers in a vase, placing them on the windowsill.

I must have been sitting there for ages. Perhaps I nodded off.

All of a sudden, the orderly reappeared, "You're still here? We're a bit short-staffed. Would you mind feeding your wife?"

I didn't bother to correct her. I simply agreed and helped the orderly sit Ellen up in the bed before adjusting the table so that it was in front of her. The orderly placed the unappetising supper on the table. It was beginning to get dark outside.

Fastening the bib around Ellen's neck I managed to feed her a few mouthfuls of the nondescript meal. But she simply refused to eat anymore. She kept her mouth shut and shook her head. I fantasised about the sort of meal I could have prepared for her at home. I'd become quite a good cook over the years.

Placing the tray on her bedside table I began talking about the past. I didn't know how much she understood or even heard but it made me feel better.

I started listing my precious memories; the smell of the blackboard when it was newly repainted at the beginning of each term. The excitement of being given a new exercise book, and the day our teacher was sick, so we were sent home early. But the best of all was the day she came to my school.

The orderly returned with the dessert. "Maybe

she'll like this. The food will take some time to get used to. It says on the menu 'Strawberry Fool.' But looks like yogurt to me."

As I spoon-fed Ellen the pink pudding a small smile appeared on her face. I wondered whether she remembered the reversal of positions. For me, even after all these years, it was as clear as yesterday when she had come to visit with her gift of strawberries while I was in bed.

When she'd finished every last bit I dabbed her face with the paper serviette. Then I placed the bowl and spoon on the table and moved it away from the bed.

Putting my coat on I went to leave. I turned to say goodbye one more time and to have one last look. She no longer gazed up above. Instead, she looked straight at me. I couldn't hear what she said so I walked slowly towards her and knelt by her bed. My knees creaked as I lowered myself down. I could feel her hot breath on my cheek as I turned my ear to her face. It took her a great deal of effort to whisper, "I'm so sorry about your legs."

© *Andrew Campbell-Kearsey*

Images licensed to Pen & Ink Designs Publishing

THE YEWS OF KINGLEY VALE

As I stand here, the whole Vale remains a strange and foreboding place; from the outside the entwined trees give little away to the eye about the woodland. Once inside the first thing is the quietness, the birds are hushed and the canopy of yew reduces the sunlight to a winter glow. Even at the height of summer, Kingley Vale feels like a deathly cold place.

Why I had returned after all these years I could not answer. But memories are strange things, especially those that cast a shadow over a lifetime. The darker ones have an unconscious life of their own; a fleeting thought or an unusual smell may turn on their ignition, sending the memory roaring into action.

I had passed the station for years but only today had the flames of memory urged me back to the Vale. More forceful was the desire to travel, as I had done all those years ago: a carriage to the past. Gazing at the reflection in the window, I had watched my car drift away just as I had watched my father wave me off from the same spot decades before.

In that moment, the two images had become one, and lurking behind them was a dreadful-looking tree. Crack went the first branch, and the second broke and tumbled to the ground. Out came the two boys, emerging like newborn chicks into the sunshine. They ruffled and shook their bodies, throwing off twigs and vines that had hitched a ride through the forest.

The Scouts had trained them well. Now the boys were full of confidence, enough to form a small group that had departed from the main camp almost an hour ago.

"I think we should carry on through the trees, follow this little path and head up to the top of the ridge. That way we can see our lot and gloat," said Tom brashly, delighted that he was now on a real adventure.

"Yes, but we shouldn't stay away too long," said Alex, feeling demoted.

"We must keep our boys in sight; make sure that no one starts to look for us. Otherwise, it'll be curtains and we'll end up shadowed for the entire trip."

"All right," agreed Tom, "let's just get up onto the ridge; then we'll circle the camp and head down the other side for a little surprise!"

The boys shared a smile, pleased with their plan.

On they went, much deeper into the woods; but as the light began to fade, fewer and fewer words were exchanged between the pair. Though neither mentioned it, both had become anxious about the darkening path ahead.

The distant echoed voices of the scout camp were now a faded memory. On they trudged, winding their way gradually through entwined roots and branches until, at last, they reached the brow of the hill.

The thinning sunlight was flickering through the treetops. Four shadowed mounds stood before them like beasts in slumber; a small chalk path snaking between their gentle slopes. The boys wearily staggered to the mound nearest them, and lifted off their heavy packs, before dropping to the ground.

There was a wild and remote feeling about the place, something that did not escape them.

"Stay the night?" said Tom sarcastically, hoping that Alex would disagree.

"Well, the choice is either we stay or we head back down through that mess of a forest," replied Alex. "The light's going and now we're definitely going to be missed. The last thing we need is a search party; then we'll be for it!"

The boys fell into a lengthy silence, staring thoughtfully out across the barrows, aware they were in an ancient place, resting amongst the dead. And with that thought, shivers pulsed through them.

"And there's another reason I'm not so keen to stay here....," said Alex, his voice trailing off with an uneasy quiver.

"O-h-h-h," teased Tom, "you're not talking about these grassy mounds are you? Those stories really got you going, didn't they?"

Alex shifted his body, visibly agitated, extending a dig of the elbow in Tom's direction.

The night before they had been entertained by their scout leader, an old wag who delighted in recounting ancient tales of terror. The ghastly deeds of ghosts and witches were made all the more chilling having been told by candlelight, the flickering of the flame highlighting the gnarled features of the surrounding yews.

One story, in particular, had captivated them. It told of Danish invaders who came to Sussex over a thousand years ago. They had travelled great distances to conquer the Saxon communities of South Britain but the locals had fought back, slaying some of the invaders in the skirmishes amongst the yew trees near Bow Hill.

Legend says that the four large barrows upon the hill, known as The Devil's Humps, are the graves of the dead Vikings. In late summer evenings, when the blood-red sap of the yews spill onto the chalk hill it is said that their ghosts roam the dark and silent wood, tormented by defeat.

"I don't care about those stories," retorted Alex sharply, "I just want to avoid a thrashing from my father!"

Though Tom laughed, his companion's comment helped make up his mind.

"Fine, let's head back down. I've got a good sense of direction and we shouldn't be too far. Besides, we should be able to spot the camp as they'll be lighting the bonfire soon."

The boys remained seated for a while longer, then reloading their backpacks they headed back in the direction they had come. However, neither was aware of the events unfolding behind them. If, at that moment, they had turned, their gaze would have fallen on something creeping out of the darkness.

The shadow of a tree was inching its way over the grass. It crawled into the folds of earth where the boys had rested, seeping into the soil, turning it a vicious blood red.

Over the brow of the hill and into the realms of darkness went the explorers, the shadow following close behind. The path they took was a minefield of hooked roots and sharp boulders, tearing their ankles at every step. Only when the orange hue of distant flames sprung up against the blackness did the boys sense with relief that they would make it back to camp.

The sight of the bonfire pushed the boys further, lifting their pace, until they came upon the ravelled limbs of a large yew tree, lying directly in their path. The companions stood for a while considering what; ultimately they could not say. So large was the tree that the distant light of the bonfire, the beacon guiding them along the torturous route, was now out of sight; the edges of the wood etched only by the thin moonlight.

Tom tried to climb the first hurdle, a thick, densely knotted branch that protruded from the mass, but his clambering was swiftly halted by an encounter with something sitting on the bark, a sticky, foul-smelling substance.

"Yuck!" shouted Tom, his hands withdrawing from the sickly-sweet liquid. "This is disgusting!"

The putrid matter clung to his hands and sparkled under the moonlight. Only when he raised his hands up to the meagre light did he catch a glimpse of colour. A rich red glow throbbed within the dappled stickiness.

"Don't come up here, it's horrible," he shouted, a warning to Alex.

"I don't think I need to," responded Alex. "It seems to be everywhere," and with that he tugged his foot, pulling hard against the sinews of the jelly-like substance anchoring his foot to the ground.

"What the hell is this?" he cried.

As Tom tried to remove himself from the recumbent branch he found he was held firmly. The redness was now bubbling up around his wrists, cementing him to the wood.

The terrified boys began to scream and shout, frantically wriggling their bodies, and squirming like two flies caught in a web.

And such a web it was, for what then appeared was a hideous shape of spider-like appearance; its armoured body flanked by pairs of limbs each armed with swords. The foul creature had crept from a hollow within the trunk and was now moving its legs in horrible synchrony, like spindle-thin oars paddling up a river.

As the thing approached, Alex realised that what he had first taken to be a single piece of metal protruding from the centre of its body was, in fact, a horrible assortment of helmets and shields, all melded together.

The more he studied the creature, the more horrified he became; for at the centre of this mass were heads - human heads – all moving, their eyes wide open; their mouths forming the shapes of unspoken words.

The boys recoiled in horror, screaming at the sky, pleading for help. But, for every shriek, the creature edged further along the wood, closer and closer towards its powerless victims.

Finally, it came upon them.

Alex and Tom could smell the stench of its body, its fetid breath, and worse still, the sight of a sea of eyes gazing down upon their quivering bodies.

The creature stood still for a moment, watching them. Then two of its arms sprang forward, each clutching swords, lowering them down to a hair's breadth of their throats. The boys shut their eyes and waited for the blades to strike. But nothing came.

Not daring to open them, they listened to the short, prying sniffs of the thing hovering above, sensing the movement of air as the swords withdrew from their throats and then there was the sound of the scuttling monster withdrawing back into its hole.

"Quick, run!" shouted Tom, aware that the red substance trapping them had returned to liquid and was flowing away down the sides of the tree. Each boy, now released, sprang from the dreadful nest and went running wildly into the woods.

The shrieks made whilst they were imprisoned had sent a search party in their direction; and now the scoutmaster, his deputy, and a group of older boys were waiting only a short distance downhill.

Little was said on the way back – the party concentrating on navigating the dense arrangement of branch and foliage - but once they had reached the camp, the boys recounted their terrible tale. The party sat in gloomy, pensive silence and listened, reflecting on the screams they had heard, but ignorant of the horrors the pair had faced.

The following morning, the scoutmaster led a small group to the area the boys described but they returned reporting seeing nothing out of the ordinary.

It has taken me sixty years before I was willing to return to the wood.

Alex remained a close friend but there was nothing I could say that would persuade him to accompany me.

As I stood in the centre of the wood I reflected on that terrible night. There had been little since to explain what had happened. But, I knew that it had, though no one apart from Alex believed it so. There were times when even I doubted that we had not convinced ourselves that it was all a nightmarish dream.

But, there was the question of why the sinful creature had withdrawn its execution; something that has plagued me all these years. Had God's goodness spared me, or was it something else?

Many times I have pondered that my being the son of a Saxon could not have been so lucky.

© *Andrew Campbell-Kearsey*

Images licensed to Pen & Ink Designs Publishing

FINANCIAL GAIN

As I sit here writing, I am drawn back in time. I can only hope that the contents of this missive, will be a warning to others who are considering taking the law into their own hands, for it can only lead to destruction; that of one's self. Here is my confession:

My name is Hannah Chesham. I am thirty-six years old, and in two days I will meet my maker. I have been found guilty of murder, most foul. And, if I am honest, then I deserve all that the law has in store for me, for I have committed the most horrendous of crimes.

Not for revenge, or in a fit of passion, but for mere financial gain - my own; and that is one of the worst reasons of all for any crime.

It isn't as though I have always been a bad person. On the contrary, I was raised by God-fearing parents. It was they who sent me to church every Sunday where I was instructed in the meaning of right and wrong. But, times change, and so do people, especially when they are left in difficult circumstances, or if they are greedy. And that was my problem; I was greedy.

I had lived a normal life, until going into service when aged seventeen. The family I worked for were not unkind,

although I did find the work exceedingly hard. The hours were long; rising at six in the morning, but not retiring until midnight. The only relief was the time I spent in church on Sunday, and the odd day off when I could go home to visit my family.

By the time I was nineteen, I was developing into a curvaceous young woman, so soon caught the eye of the eldest son of the house. He was a lecherous man. It took all of my ingenuity to avoid being alone with him. But, in time, his attention increased, leaving me with no option but to find a new position. And so, I found myself having to move away from the area. I chose to make my way to London, which was probably my first mistake. Yet, I knew that if I were to stay, then the son would dishonour me.

Living in the big city wasn't as easy as I thought it would be. Soon, I found myself caught up with the wrong sort of people. My fears of the sons' advances were soon put into the shade, as I found myself drawn into a life of prostitution; this being the only way to survive.

It hadn't been my intention to go down this road, but sometimes the means must. I was mixing with the low life of London, which was not what I had planned, and it came to a point where I knew I must escape the terrible life I was now embroiled in.

And so, it was by accident that I changed careers.

Within days of making this decision, I met a young woman named Mary Smith. She was, at that time, living with a man called George, who was much older than her. At the beginning of their relationship, he had been kind and caring but, over time, he had become violent. Mary had only remained with him, as he had an income of five hundred pounds a year.

A few weeks later, Mary came to see me; she was crying. Once she had calmed down, she explained how George had changed, and how he was threatening to throw her out into the street. She didn't know what to do, asking if I had any ideas.

This was my second mistake.

After much discussion we devised a plan that would get rid of George once and for all, leaving Mary free to do whatever she wanted.

With the plan hatched, Mary was to return home and prepare a delightful meal. In the meantime, I would go to the apothecary and purchase some arsenic powder. I had heard somewhere that arsenic could be used to rid oneself of fleas and bedbugs. However, it was also poisonous, and if ingested would result in death. We had agreed she would poison George. Afterwards, I would give her an alibi, and in return, Mary promised to share with me whatever funds there were in the house.

That evening I joined the couple for dinner; eating the same food as everyone else. However, Mary and I did not drink any of the wine. After George and his manservant had retired for the night, I took the wine bottle and destroyed it; replacing it with another of a similar kind, filled to the same level. I quickly washed the glass George had drunk from and then partly filled it with some of the replacement wine. After which, Mary and I retired for the night.

Sometime during the night, we were woken by the servant informing us that his Master was asking for Mary as he didn't feel well. She left the room, and upon entering his bedroom discovered George doubled over. He was vomiting violently, whilst trying to cope with bouts of diarrhoea. Although the scene was unpleasant, Mary did what she could for the poor man.

As morning approached, and there was no improvement, I suggested to the manservant that he fetch medical help. But, by the time the doctor arrived, George was breathing his last.

Much later, after the doctor left, the constable arrived. All three of us were rigorously questioned; the manservant confirming we had all eaten the same food. Spying the half-empty glass and wine bottle on the dining table, the constable took them away to be tested. The results were,

of course, clear, and once all things were settled, Mary, being accepted as the 'spouse' of the deceased, finally received all of George's belongings. Being delighted with the outcome she kept her promise, and duly shared the assets with me.

It was from that moment on, that Mary and I

became the closest of friends.

The ease with which one could buy arsenic gave us an idea of how we could improve our financial position, and so we began looking at ways in which we could take care of our future well-being.

We calculated, that as long as we only bought small amounts of arsenic once a month, we would be able to put our plan into action. Firstly, we chose a different apothecary each time to buy the lethal dose from. Going to the apothecary, we would complain about fleas, bedbugs, or rats, asking the man what he recommended we could do about them. When it was suggested we use arsenic, we acted in all innocence, as if we had never heard of the method before.

The successful disposal of an unwanted victim meant Mary and I lived the highlife but, of course, in time the funds would run out. It was at this moment that we planned to find a new victim.

There were certain requirements for this.

First, the person must be old. He also had to be wealthy. Plus, he had to be willing to accept either one of us into his home. It was also preferable that he lived alone, with no relatives.

It didn't take us long to line up our next victim; Henry.

Dear Henry was in his sixties but he loved the high life. Mary soon ingratiated herself into his company, and he in turn became quite smitten with her. He had an income of three hundred and fifty pounds a year and owned a house, but he was also a bit of a recluse. Mary worked her wiles upon him, whilst Henry ignored all the warnings from his few friends. Whenever they visited she would make sure she was always pleasant to them; acting coy and bashful. In time, they too began to believe she was just an innocent girl, down on her luck.

After about two months, I was invited to move into the house. I pretended to be Mary's sister, as well as a cook., Although reluctant at first, having two young women waiting on him hand and foot, made Henry soon find the idea quite satisfactory. And so, we all lived amicably together for some three months. That was until Mary decided she wanted to end the farce, and so we made our plans to dispose of Henry, as soon as possible.

With the season drawing to a close, Henry's friends had retired to their country estates, meaning visitors to the house were drastically reduced. About two weeks later, Henry became unwell. Because he didn't drink alcohol, I had to doctor the food. Henry loved eggs for breakfast but Mary didn't, so I laced the egg tray with arsenic. As soon as the meal was over, I removed the tray, disposed of any leftover eggs, and washed the tray before refilling it with two freshly cooked eggs, which I left on one side. By the time I had finished, Henry had taken to his bed with sickness.

Cruelly, we let him suffer for about three hours before finally sending for the doctor. Of course, being the time of year, it was hard to find one readily available, thus it took another hour before the man finally arrived. At the house, he discovered a distressed Mary pacing up and down. She acted her part perfectly, leaving the doctor with no suspicion that anything was wrong. Poor Henry passed away shortly afterwards.

The constable, having been called, checked the left-over eggs before declaring that Henry must have died from a stomach bug. This was something quite common in town, especially during the warmer summer months. Yet again, Mary inherited the assets of the deceased; this time legally, as Henry had named her in his will as his sole heir.

When Henry's friends returned for the funeral, they began questioning the circumstances of his passing. This caused us some concern, so we decided to leave the area as soon as it was decently possible to do so.

With the success of George and Henry's demise, Mary and I decided to lay low for a short time. After much discussion, we realised we had to be very careful how we chose our next victim. This time we would take our time to ensure we created a strong relationship with him. We had spent only a few months with Henry, and with his friends being suspicious of the situation, we knew we couldn't allow anyone to ask the wrong questions in the future.

As it turned out, we didn't need to find our next victim for he found us; or at least his wife did. I am not sure how we got on to the subject, but Clara was crying woefully about how cruel her husband was. Before I realised what was happening, Mary had offered to help dispose of him, on condition that the wife paid us. She readily agreed, and before I could prevent it, we were discussing how it would be done.

This, was mistake number three; involving someone else.

Plans were put into place, and within six weeks the husband was dead with the widow paying us the agreed sum. This proved to be our first step into the murder business, and the start of the downward spiral in our characters.

Over time, the awareness of arsenic poisoning became more recognised. This meant we found ourselves having to be more careful with our plans. Unfortunately, even though the number of trials held at the Old Bailey for murder by poisoning, increased threefold, the monetary gain was too big an attraction. It appeared that poisoning had become an easy option for women who wanted to be rid of their spouses or other family members. After all, they cooked, looked after the house and, of course, cared for the sick. Arsenic was now being used for a multitude of problems, meaning that no house was without at least one small packet of the stuff.

However, eventually, all good things must come to an end.

Expertise in toxicology was growing, and the discovery of arsenic in bodies became more prominent and recognisable.

There was also an increase in the public outcry at the number of deaths caused by arsenic poisoning; whether accidental or intentional. And so, in time the Government chose to bring in a new legislation regarding the sale of the stuff. This meant that no one could buy it without giving proof of who they were, and what they needed it for.

These very records would be the result of our downfall.

Following the death of our most recent victim, it was only after some bright person decided to cross-reference the buyer's names recorded that the pattern of our purchases was discovered. And so, shortly afterwards, Mary and I were both taken into custody. Following a court case, and despite our declaring ourselves innocent, the judge found us both guilty, sentencing us to death by hanging.

Fortunately for Mary, it was discovered she was pregnant. The courts will not hand down a death sentence to any woman who is with child. Mary is therefore going to be transported tomorrow to the new land called Australia. Neither of us is sure if she has the easier of the two sentences for the new land is many, many miles away.

We have been fortunate to be able to say our goodbyes to one another. The journey my friend is about to undertake is long and arduous. Whether she and the child will survive, I do not know but, I pray to God that he will look upon her kindly and that she can be forgiven for the wrongs she has committed.

As for me, I have been told that in two days I will be taken to the scaffold and hung. I confess I am afraid; but then who wouldn't be?

And so, this is my tale, or I should say, my confession. I hope that this record when shown to people, will teach them to learn from my terrible mistakes. And that they will remember that the high life isn't always worth the cost.

Now, I can only hope that God may have mercy upon my Soul.

© *Robina Brooks*

ABOUT PEN & INK DESIGNS PUBLISHING

Pen & Ink Designs began in 2002, and worked with the Kids4Kids UK organisation, the acting name of the John Hardy Trust Charity. The charity was set up to benefit youngsters through the element of sport. After the Trust closed Pen & Ink Designs moved into publishing to continue their journey of helping youngsters, but this time through the element of writing.

With the aid of Kids4Kids we mentored and published a number of select books by younger writers and continue to do so to this day.

In 2013 & 2014 we ran our first two writing competitions. The original version of this book was the result.

Since then we have developed Mentoring Writers which assists writers worldwide, over the age of 17, to achieve their goal and ambition of becoming a writer/author.

Mentoring Writers has held further writing competitions, producing three anthologies. One for children and two for adult readers all consisting of short stories and/or poetry.

For details of our other authors books check out the

Pen & Ink Designs website

www.penandinkdesigns.co.uk

www.mentoringwriters.co.uk

www.kids4kids.org.uk

QR CODES

www.penandinkdesigns.co.uk

 www.mentoringwriters.co.uk

www.kids4kids.org.uk

www.ingramcontent.com/pod-product-compliance
Lightning Source LLC
Chambersburg PA
CBHW042144170626
46815CB00006BA/305